LONGMAN IMPRINT BOOKS

Stories Old and New

Contrasts from two centuries

Selected and edited by Geoff Barton

General editor: Michael Marland
Series consultant: Geoff Barton

D0301274

Contents

CONTENTS

The National Curriculum

The National Curriculum for English says that pupils should read literature 'drawn from a variety of genres, including plays, novels, short stories and poetry'. It names such authors as Charles Dickens, Elizabeth Gaskell, Graham Greene and D. H. Lawrence. All are represented here – plus a host of other major short-story writers.

It says that short stories should 'include a range of narrative structures and techniques'; 'extend pupils' ideas and their moral and emotional understanding'; 'offer perspectives on society and community and their impact on the lives of individuals': and 'show the variety of language use in fiction'. *Stories Old and New* has been compiled to do all these things.

The book also aims to give readers opportunities to explore social and historical contexts of literature, to compare texts, and to use these explorations as the basis of lively, imaginative coursework assignments.

Comparing the texts

Grouped by social and historical context

1850–1900
The Tell-Tale Heart (1840s), *The Half-Brothers* (1850s), *The Signalman* (1860s)

1900–1950
A Lesson on a Tortoise (1910s), *The Voyage* (1920s), *The Wounded Cormorant* (1920s), *The Case for the Defence* (1930s), *The Dress* (1930s)

1950– present
The Raffle (1950s), *The Elephant Man* (1960s), *Next Term, We'll Mash You* (1970s), *Through the Tunnel* (1970s), *Bang, Bang – Who's Dead?* (1980s)

Comparison of theme and content

The Dress and *The Half-Brothers*
Through the Tunnel and *Next Term, We'll Mash You*

Comparison of style and language

The Signalman and *The Tell-Tale Heart*
A Lesson on a Tortoise and *The Voyage*

Introduction

Stories Old and New contains short stories from some of our finest writers. It ranges from the mid-nineteenth century to our own day, and embraces writers from Britain, Ireland, Trinidad, Africa and New Zealand.

Short stories have their roots in the oral tradition – people gathering together to tell one another tales at a single sitting. When the ability to read was the privilege of a learned minority, stories were memorised, told and retold. The short story as a written form has fairly modern roots. There are hints of it, perhaps, in some of the stories of the Bible, and in Chaucer's fourteenth-century *Canterbury Tales*. But the short story we recognise today did not begin to develop until late in the nineteenth century.

In Britain the huge three-volume novel dominated, giving a reading experience which must in some ways have been similar to today's soap operas. Narratives were structured around a variety of characters, with main story-lines and sub-plots. It was a form which satisfied the appetite of many readers for large-scale story-telling, but some disliked it. Edgar Allan Poe said that the novel cannot have the powerful emotional impact of a short story because it cannot be read all at one go.

By the twentieth century the short story was established as a literary form which most major writers seem to have explored. It has flourished in Ireland and, since about 1950, it has become a significant form in West Indian literature.

Part of the special appeal of the short story is that it can transport us to a way of life far removed from our own. For example, Penelope Lively's *Next Term, We'll Mash You* describes a school which is probably far removed from the one you attend – and yet its themes of fear, snobbery and cruelty feel powerfully familiar. Whether a story is old or new, familiar or unknown, it has a special capacity to make us see through other eyes. Where a novel might concern itself with establishing a range of characters, creating strong, physical settings and constructing sub-plots, the short story works with a lighter touch. Details, hints, fragments of conversation, things left unsaid – these are the powerful tools of the short-story writer. And, as a result, the form can deliver a kind of emotional blow that may linger in the mind for weeks.

It would have been tempting to organise this book in a chronological sequence – putting the oldest story first, then the next, until we arrived breathless at the present day. But my aim was to show how stories work when placed side by side, how the theme of one illuminates another. I have therefore grouped stories together to provoke comparisons and contrasts: for example, how do writers show the minds of two villains? I have avoided using themes like 'Childhood' because they limit our response to texts – a story which for one person might be about childhood may, for another reader, be about cruelty.

As you read the stories I hope that you will focus not only on what the stories are about, but on the way they are written; most of all, that you will go on to read more short stories for pleasure, and create your own groupings of stories old and new.

Geoff Barton

A Lesson on a Tortoise

by D. H. Lawrence

It was the last lesson on Friday afternoon, and this, with Standard VI, was Nature Study from half-past three till half-past four. The last lesson of the week is a weariness to teachers and scholars. It is the end; there is no need to keep up the tension of discipline and effort any longer, and, yielding to weariness, a teacher is spent.

But Nature Study is a pleasant lesson. I had got a big old tortoise, who had not yet gone to sleep, though November was darkening the early afternoon, and I knew the boys would enjoy sketching him. I put him under the radiator to warm while I went for a large empty shell that I had sawn in two to show the ribs of some ancient tortoise absorbed in his bony coat. When I came back I found Joe, the old reptile, stretching slowly his skinny neck, and looking with indifferent eyes at the two intruding boys who were kneeling beside him. I was too good-tempered to send them out again into the playground, too slack with the great relief of Friday afternoon. So I bade them put out the Nature books ready. I crouched to look at Joey, and stroked his horny, blunt head with my finger. He was quite lively. He spread out his legs and gripped the floor with his flat hand-like paws, then he slackened again as if from a yawn, dropping his head meditatively.

I felt pleased with myself, knowing that the boys would be delighted with the lesson. 'He will not want to walk,' I said to myself, 'and if he takes a sleepy stride, they'll be just in ecstasy, and I can easily calm him down to his old position.' So I anticipated their entry. At the end of playtime I went to bring them in. They were a small class of about thirty – my own boys. A difficult, mixed class, they were, consisting of six London Home boys, five boys from a fairly well-to-do Home for the children of actors, and a set of commoners varying from poor lads who hobbled to school, crippled by broken enormous boots, to boys who brought soft, light shoes to wear in school on snowy days. The Gordons were a difficult set; you could pick them out: crop haired, coarsely dressed lads, distrustful, always ready to assume the defensive. They would lie till it made my heart sick, if they were charged with offence, but they were willing, and would respond beautifully to an appeal. The actors were of different fibre: some gentle, a pleasure even to look at; others polite and obedient, but indifferent, covertly insolent and vulgar; all of them more or less gentlemanly.

The boys crowded round the table noisily as soon as they discovered Joe. 'Is he alive? – Look, his head's coming out! He'll bite you? – He *won't*!' – with much scorn – 'Please Sir, do tortoises bite?' I hurried them off to their seats in a little group in front, and pulled the table up to the desks. Joe kept fairly still. The boys nudged each other excitedly, making half audible remarks concerning the poor reptile, looking quickly from me to Joe and then to their neighbours. I set them sketching, but in their pleasure at the novelty they could not be still:

'Please Sir – shall we draw the marks on the shell? Please Sir, has he only got four toes?' – 'Toes!' echoes somebody, covertly delighted at the absurdity of calling the grains of claws 'toes'. 'Please Sir, he's moving – Please Sir!'

I stroked his neck and calmed him down:

'Now don't make me wish I hadn't brought him. That's enough. Miles – you shall go to the back and draw twigs if I hear you again! Enough now – be still, get on with the drawing, it's hard!'

I wanted peace for myself. They began to sketch diligently. I stood and looked across at the sunset, which I could see facing me through my window, a great gold sunset, very large and magnificent, rising up in immense gold beauty beyond the town, that was become a low dark strip of nothingness under the wonderful up-building of the western sky. The light, the thick, heavy golden sunlight which is only seen in its full dripping splendour in town, spread on the desks and the floor like gold lacquer. I lifted my hands, to take the sunlight on them, smiling faintly to myself, trying to shut my fingers over its tangible richness.

'Please Sir!' – I was interrupted – 'Please Sir, can we have rubbers?'

The question was rather plaintive. I had said they should have rubbers no more. I could not keep my stock, I could not detect the thief among them, and I was weary of the continual degradation of bullying them to try to recover what was lost among them. But it was Friday afternoon, very peaceful and happy. Like a bad teacher, I went back on my word:

'Well –!' I said, indulgently.

My monitor, a pale, bright, erratic boy, went to the cupboard and took out a red box.

'Please Sir!' he cried, then he stopped and counted again in the box. 'Eleven! There's only eleven, Sir, and there were fifteen when I put them away on Wednesday –!'

The class stopped, every face upturned. Joe sunk, and lay flat on his shell, his leg limp. Another of the

3

hateful moments had come. The sunset was smeared out, the charm of the afternoon was smashed like a fair glass that falls to the floor. My nerves seemed to tighten, and to vibrate with sudden tension.

'Again!' I cried, turning to the class in passion, to the upturned faces, and the sixty watchful eyes.

'Again! I am sick of it, sick of it, I am! A thieving, wretched set! – a skulking, mean lot!' I was quivering with anger and distress.

'Who is it? You must know! You are all as bad as one another, you hide it – a miserable –!' I looked round the class in great agitation. The 'Gordons' with their distrustful faces, were noticeable:

'Marples!' I cried to one of them, 'where are those rubbers?'

'I don't know where they are – I've never 'ad no rubbers' – he almost shouted back, with the usual insolence of his set. I was more angry:

'You must know! They're gone – they don't melt into air, they don't fly – who took them then? Rawson, do you know anything of them?'

'No Sir!' he cried, with impudent indignation.

'No, you intend to know nothing! Wood, have you any knowledge of these four rubbers?'

'No!' he shouted, with absolute insolence.

'Come here!' I cried, 'come here! Fetch the cane, Burton. We'll make an end, insolence and thieving and all.'

The boy dragged himself to the front of the class, and stood slackly, almost crouching, glaring at me. The rest of the 'Gordons' sat upright in their desks, like animals of a pack ready to spring. There was tense silence for a moment. Burton handed me the cane, and I turned from the class to Wood. I liked him best among the Gordons.

'Now my lad!' I said. 'I'll cane you for impudence first.'

He turned swiftly to me; tears sprang to his eyes.

'Well,' he shouted at me, 'you always pick on the Gordons – you're always on to us –!' This was so manifestly untrue that my anger fell like a bird shot in a midflight.

'Why!' I exclaimed, 'what a disgraceful untruth! I am always excusing you, letting you off –!'

'But you pick on us – you start on us – you pick on Marples, an' Rawson, an' on me. You always begin with the Gordons.'

'Well,' I answered, justifying myself, 'isn't it natural? Haven't you boys stolen – haven't these boys stolen – several times – and been caught?'

'That doesn't say as we do now,' he replied.

'How am I to know? You don't help me. How do I know? Isn't it natural to suspect you –?'

'Well, it's not us. We know who it is. Everybody knows who it is – only they won't tell.'

'Who know?' I asked.

'Why Rawson, and Maddock, and Newling, and all of 'em.'

I asked these boys if they could tell me. Each one shook his head, and said 'No Sir.' I went round the class. It was the same. They lied to me every one.

'You see,' I said to Wood.

'Well – they won't own up,' he said. 'I shouldn't 'a done if you hadn't 'a been goin' to cane me.'

This frankness was painful, but I preferred it. I made them all sit down. I asked Wood to write his knowledge on a piece of paper, and I promised not to divulge. He would not. I asked the boys he had named, all of them. They refused. I asked them again – I appealed to them.

'Let them all do it then!' said Wood. I tore up scraps of paper, and gave each boy one.

'Write on it the name of the boy you suspect. He is a thief and a sneak. He gives endless pain and trouble to us all. It is your duty.'

They wrote furtively, and quickly doubled up the papers. I collected them in the lid of the rubber box, and sat at the table to examine them. There was dead silence, they all watched me. Joe had withdrawn into his shell, forgotten.

A few papers were blank; several had 'I suspect nobody' – these I threw in the paper basket; two had the name of an old thief, and these I tore up; eleven bore the name of my assistant monitor a splendid, handsome boy, one of the oldest of the actors. I remembered how deferential and polite he had been when I had asked him, how ready to make barren suggestions; I remembered his shifty, anxious look during the questioning; I remembered how eager he had been to do things for me before the monitor came in the room. I knew it was he – without remembering.

'Well!' I said, feeling very wretched when I was convinced that the papers were right. 'Go on with the drawing.'

They were very uneasy and restless, but quiet. From time to time they watched me. Very shortly, the bell rang. I told the two monitors to collect up the things, and I sent the class home. We did not go into prayers. I, and they, were in no mood for hymns and the evening prayer of gratitude.

When the monitors had finished, and I had turned out all the lights but one, I sent home Curwen, and kept my assistant monitor a moment.

'Ségar, do you know anything of my rubbers?'

'No Sir' – he had a deep, manly voice, and he spoke with earnest protestation – flushing.

'No? Nor my pencils – nor my two books?'

'No Sir! I know nothing about the books.'

'No? the pencils then –?'

'No Sir! Nothing! I don't know anything about them.'

'Nothing, Ségar?'

'No Sir.'

He hung his head, and looked so humiliated, a fine, handsome lad, that I gave it up. Yet I knew he would be dishonest again, when the opportunity arrived.

'Very well! You will not help as monitor any more. You will not come into the classroom until the class comes in – any more. You understand?'

'Yes Sir' – he was very quiet.

'Go along then.'

He went out, and silently closed the door. I turned out the last light, tried the cupboards, and went home.

I felt very tired, and very sick. The night had come up, the clouds were moving darkly, and the sordid streets near the school felt like disease in the lamplight.

The Raffle

by V. S. Naipaul

They don't pay primary schoolteachers a lot in Trinidad, but they allow them to beat their pupils as much as they want.

Mr Hinds, my teacher, was a big beater. On the shelf below *The Last of England* he kept four or five tamarind rods.[1] They are good for beating. They are limber, they sting and they last. There was a tamarind tree in the schoolyard. In his locker Mr Hinds also kept a leather strap soaking in the bucket of water every class had in case of fire.

It wouldn't have been so bad if Mr Hinds hadn't been so young and athletic. At the one school sports I went to, I saw him slip off his shining shoes, roll up his trousers neatly to mid-shin and win the Teachers' Hundred Yards, a cigarette between his lips, his tie flapping smartly over his shoulder. It was a wine-coloured tie: Mr Hinds was careful about his dress. That was something else that somehow added to the terror. He wore a brown suit, a cream shirt and the wine-coloured tie.

It was also rumoured that he drank heavily at weekends.

But Mr Hinds had a weak spot. He was poor. We knew he gave those 'private lessons' because he needed the extra money. He gave us private lessons in the ten-

[1] rods made from the wood of a tropical evergreen tree

minute morning recess. Every boy paid fifty cents for that. If a boy didn't pay, he was kept in all the same and flogged until he paid.

We also knew that Mr Hinds had an allotment in Morvant where he kept some poultry and a few animals.

The other boys sympathised with us – needlessly. Mr Hinds beat us, but I believe we were all a little proud of him.

I say he beat us, but I don't really mean that. For some reason which I could never understand then and can't now, Mr Hinds never beat me. He never made me clean the blackboard. He never made me shine his shoes with the duster. He even called me by my first name, Vidiadhar.

This didn't do me any good with the other boys. At cricket I wasn't allowed to bowl or keep wicket and I always went in at number eleven. My consolation was that I was spending only two terms at the school before going on to Queen's Royal College. I didn't want to go to QRC so much as I wanted to get away from Endeavour (that was the name of the school). Mr Hinds's favour made me feel insecure.

At private lessons one morning Mr Hinds announced that he was going to raffle a goat – a shilling a chance.

He spoke with a straight face and nobody laughed. He made me write out the names of all the boys in the class on two foolscap sheets. Boys who wanted to risk a shilling had to put a tick after their names. Before private lessons ended there was a tick after every name.

I became very unpopular. Some boys didn't believe there was a goat. They all said that if there was a goat, they knew who was going to get it. I hoped they were right. I had long wanted an animal of my own, and the idea of getting milk from my own goat attracted me. I had heard that Mannie Ramjohn, Trinidad's champion miler, trained on goat's milk and nuts.

Next morning I wrote out the names of the boys on slips of paper. Mr Hinds borrowed my cap, put the slips in, took one out, said 'Vidiadhar, is your goat,' and immediately threw all the slips into the wastepaper basket.

At lunch I told my mother, 'I win a goat today.'

'What sort of goat?'

'I don't know. I ain't see it.'

She laughed. She didn't believe in the goat, either. But when she finished laughing she said: 'It would be nice, though.'

I was getting not to believe in the goat, too. I was afraid to ask Mr Hinds, but a day or two later he said, 'Vidiadhar, you coming or you ain't coming to get your goat?'

He lived in a tumbledown wooden house in Woodbrook and when I got there I saw him in khaki shorts, vest and blue canvas shoes. He was cleaning his bicycle with a yellow flannel. I was overwhelmed. I had never associated him with such dress and such a menial labour. But his manner was more ironic and dismissing than in the classroom.

He led me to the back of the yard. There *was* a goat. A white one with big horns, tied to a plum tree. The ground around the tree was filthy. The goat looked sullen and sleepy-eyed, as if a little stunned by the smell it had made. Mr Hinds invited me to stroke the goat. I stroked it. He closed his eyes and went on chewing. When I stopped stroking him, he opened his eyes.

Every afternoon at about five an old man drove a donkey-cart through Miguel Street where we lived. The cart was piled with fresh grass tied into neat little bundles, so neat you felt grass wasn't a thing that grew but was made in a factory somewhere. That donkey-cart became important to my mother and me. We were buying five, sometimes six bundles a day, and every bundle cost six cents. The goat didn't change. He still looked sullen and bored. From time to time Mr Hinds asked me with a smile how the goat was getting on, and I said it was getting on fine. But when I asked my mother when we were going to get milk from the goat she told me to stop aggravating her. Then one day she put up a sign:

RAM FOR SERVICE
Apply Within For Terms

and got very angry when I asked her to explain it.

The sign made no difference. We bought the neat bundles of grass, the goat ate, and I saw no milk.

And when I got home one lunch-time I saw no goat.

'Somebody borrow it,' my mother said. She looked happy.

'When it coming back?'

She shrugged her shoulders.

It came back that afternoon. When I turned the corner into Miguel Street I saw it on the pavement outside our house. A man I didn't know was holding it by a rope and making a big row, gesticulating like anything with his free hand. I knew that sort of man. He wasn't going to let hold of the rope until he had said his piece. A lot of people were looking on through curtains.

'But why all-you want to rob poor people so?' he said, shouting. He turned to his audience behind the curtains. 'Look, all-you, just look at this goat!'

The goat limitlessly impassive, chewed slowly, its eyes half-closed.

'But how all you people so advantageous? My brother

stupid and he ain't know this goat but I know this goat. Everybody in Trinidad who know about goat know this goat, from Icacos to Mayaro to Toco to Chaguaramas,' he said, naming the four corners of Trinidad. 'Is the most uselessest goat in the whole world. And you charge my brother for this goat? Look, you better give me back my brother money, you hear.'

My mother looked hurt and upset. She went inside and came out with some dollar notes. The man took them and handed over the goat.

That evening my mother said, 'Go and tell your Mr Hinds that I don't want this goat here.'

Mr Hinds didn't look surprised. 'Don't want it, eh?' He thought, and passed a well-trimmed thumb-nail over his moustache. 'Look, tell you. Going to buy him back. Five dollars.'

I said, 'He eat more than that in grass alone.'

That didn't surprise him either. 'Say six, then.'

I sold. That, I thought, was the end of that.

One Monday afternoon about a month before the end of my last term I announced to my mother, 'That goat raffling again.'

She became alarmed.

At tea on Friday I said casually, 'I win the goat.'

She was expecting it. Before the sun set a man had brought the goat away from Mr Hinds, given my mother some money and taken the goat away.

I hoped Mr Hinds would never ask about the goat. He did, though. Not the next week, but the week after that, just before school broke up.

I didn't know what to say.

But a boy called Knolly, a fast bowler and a favourite victim of Mr Hinds, answered for me. 'What goat?' he whispered loudly. 'That goat kill and eat long time.'

Mr Hinds was suddenly furious. 'Is true, Vidiadhar?'

I didn't nod or say anything. The bell rang and saved me.

At lunch I told my mother, 'I don't want to go back to that school.'

She said, 'You must be brave.'

I didn't like the argument, but went.

We had Geography the first period.

'Naipaul,' Mr Hinds said right away, forgetting my first name, 'define a peninsula.'

'Peninsula,' I said, 'a piece of land entirely surrounded by water.'

'Good. Come up here.' He went to the locker and took out the soaked leather strap. Then he fell on me. 'You sell my goat?' Cut. 'You kill my goat?' Cut. 'How you so damn ungrateful?' Cut, cut, cut. 'Is the last time you win anything I raffle.'

It was the last day I went to that school.

Next Term, We'll Mash You

by Penelope Lively

Inside the car it was quiet, the noise of the engine even and subdued, the air just the right temperature, the windows tight-fitting. The boy sat on the back seat, a box of chocolates, unopened, beside him, and a comic, folded. The trim Sussex landscape flowed past the windows: cows, white-fenced fields, highly priced period houses. The sunlight was glassy, remote as a coloured photograph. The backs of the two heads in front of him swayed with the motion of the car.

His mother half-turned to speak to him. 'Nearly there now, darling.'

The father glanced downwards at his wife's wrist. 'Are we all right for time?'

'Just right. Nearly twelve.'

'I could do with a drink. Hope they lay something on.'

'I'm sure they will. The Wilcoxes say they're awfully nice people. Not really the schoolmaster-type at all, Sally says.'

The man said, 'He's an Oxford chap.'

'Is he? You didn't say.'

'Mmn.'

'Of course, the fees are that much higher than the Seaford place.'

'Fifty quid or so. We'll have to see.'

The car turned right, between white gates and high, dark, tight-clipped hedges. The whisper of the road under the tyres changed to the crunch of gravel. The child, staring sideways, read black lettering on a white board: 'St Edward's Preparatory School. Please Drive Slowly.' He shifted on the seat, and the leather sucked at the bare skin under his knees, stinging.

The mother said, 'It's a lovely place. Those must be the playing-fields. Look, darling, there are some of the boys.' She clicked open her handbag, and the sun caught her mirror and flashed in the child's eyes; the comb went through her hair and he saw the grooves it left, neat as distant ploughing.

'Come on, then, Charles, out you get.'

The building was red brick, early nineteenth-century, spreading out long arms in which windows glittered blackly. Flowers, trapped in neat beds, were alternate red and white. They went up the steps, the man, the woman, and the child two paces behind.

The woman, the mother, smoothing down a skirt that would be ridged from sitting, thought: I like the way they've got the maid all done up properly. The little white apron and all that. She's foreign, I suppose. Au pair. Very nice. If he comes here there'll be Speech Days and that kind of thing. Sally Wilcox says it's quite dressy – she got that cream linen coat for coming down here. You can see why it costs a bomb. Great big grounds and only an hour and a half from London.

They went into a room looking out into a terrace. Beyond, dappled lawns, gently shifting trees, black and white cows grazing behind iron railings. Books, leather chairs, a table with magazines – *Country Life, The Field, The Economist*. 'Please, if you would wait here. The Headmaster won't be long.'

Alone, they sat, inspected. 'I like the atmosphere, don't you, John?'

'Very pleasant, yes.' Four hundred a term, near

enough. You can tell it's a cut above the Seaford place, though, or the one at St Albans. Bob Wilcox says quite a few City people send their boys here. One or two of the merchant bankers, those kind of people. It's the sort of contact that would do no harm at all. You meet someone, get talking at a cricket match or what have you ... Not at all a bad thing.

'All right, Charles? You didn't get sick in the car, did you?'

The child had black hair, slicked down smooth to his head. His ears, too large, jutted out, transparent in the light from the window, laced with tiny, delicate veins. His clothes had the shine and crease of newness. He looked at the books, the dark brown pictures, his parents, said nothing.

'Come here, let me tidy your hair.'

The door opened. The child hesitated, stood up, sat, then rose again with his father.

'Mr and Mrs Manders? How very nice to meet you – I'm Margaret Spokes, and will you please forgive my husband who is tied up with some wretch who broke the cricket pavilion window and will be just a few more minutes. We try to be organised but a schoolmaster's day is always just that bit unpredictable. Do please sit down and what will you have to revive you after that beastly drive? You live in Finchley, is that right?'

'Hampstead, really,' said the mother. 'Sherry would be lovely.' She worked over the headmaster's wife from shoes to hairstyle, pricing and assessing. Shoes old but expensive – Russell and Bromley. Good skirt. Blouse could be Marks and Sparks – not sure. Real pearls. Super Victorian ring. She's not gone to any particular trouble – that's just what she'd wear anyway. You can be confident, with a choice like that, of course. Sally Wilcox says she knows all sorts of people.

The headmaster's wife said, 'I don't know how much you know about us. Prospectuses don't tell you a thing, do they? We'll look round everything in a minute, when you've had a chat with my husband. I gather you're friends of the Wilcoxes, by the way. I'm awfully fond of Simon – he's down for Winchester,[1] of course, but I expect you know that.'

The mother smiled over her sherry. Oh, I know that all right. Sally Wilcox doesn't let you forget that.

'And this is Charles? My dear, we've been forgetting all about you! In a minute I'm going to borrow Charles and take him off to meet some of the boys because after all you're choosing a school for him, aren't you, and not for you, so he ought to know what he might be letting himself in for and it shows we've got nothing to hide.'

The parents laughed. The father, sherry warming his guts, thought that this was an amusing woman. Not attractive, of course, a bit homespun, but impressive all the same. Partly the voice, of course; it takes a bloody expensive education to produce a voice like that. And other things, of course. Background and all that stuff.

'I think I can hear the thud of the Fourth Form coming in from games, which means my husband is on the way, and then I shall leave you with him while I take Charles off to the common-room.'

For a moment the three adults centred on the child, looking, judging. The mother said, 'He looks so hideously pale, compared to those boys we saw outside.'

'My dear, that's London, isn't it? You just have to get them out, to get some colour into them. Ah, here's James. James – Mr and Mrs Manders. You remember, Bob Wilcox was mentioning at Sports Day ...'

[1] Winchester College, England's oldest public school

The headmaster reflected his wife's style, like paired cards in Happy Families. His clothes were mature rather than old, his skin well-scrubbed, his shoes clean, his geniality untainted by the least condescension. He was genuinely sorry to have kept them waiting, but in this business one lurches from one minor crisis to the next ... And this is Charles? Hello, there, Charles. His large hand rested for a moment on the child's head, quite extinguishing the thin, dark hair. It was as though he had but to clench his fingers to crush the skull. But he took his hand away and moved the parents to the window, to observe the mutilated cricket pavilion, with indulgent laughter.

And the child is borne away by the headmaster's wife. She never touches him or tells him to come, but simply bears him away like some relentless tide, down corridors and through swinging glass doors, towing him like a frail craft, not bothering to look back to see if he is following, confident in the strength of magnetism, or obedience.

And delivers him to a room where boys are scattered among inky tables and rungless chairs and sprawled on a mangy carpet. There is a scampering, and a rising, and a silence falling, as she opens the door.

'Now this is the Lower Third, Charles, who you'd be with if you come to us in September. Boys, this is Charles Manders, and I want you to tell him all about things and answer any questions he wants to ask. You can believe about half of what they say, Charles, and they will tell you the most fearful lies about the food, which is excellent.'

The boys laugh and groan; amiable, exaggerated groans. They must like the headmaster's wife: there is licensed repartee. They look at her with bright eyes in open, eager faces. Someone leaps to hold the door for her, and close it behind her. She is gone.

The child stands in the centre of the room, and it draws in around him. The circle of children contracts, faces are only a yard or so from him; strange faces, looking, assessing.

Asking questions. They help themselves to his name, his age, his school. Over their heads he sees beyond the window an inaccessible world of shivering trees and high racing clouds and his voice which has floated like a feather in the dusty schoolroom air dies altogether and he becomes mute, and he stands in the middle of them with shoulders humped, staring down at feet: grubby plimsolls and kicked brown sandals. There is a noise in his ears like rushing water, a torrential din out of which voices boom, blotting each other out so that he cannot always hear the words. Do you? they say, and Have you? and What's your? and the faces, if he looks up, swing into one another in kaleidoscopic patterns and the floor under his feet is unsteady, lifting and falling.

And out of the noises comes one voice that is complete, that he can hear. 'Next term, we'll mash you,' it says. 'We always mash new boys.'

And a bell goes, somewhere beyond doors and down corridors, and suddenly the children are all gone, clattering away and leaving him there with the heaving floor and the walls that shift and swing, and the headmaster's wife comes back and tows him away, and he is with his parents again, and they are getting into the car, and the high hedges skim past the car windows once more, in the other direction, and the gravel under the tyres changes to black tarmac.

'Well?'

'I liked it, didn't you?' The mother adjusted the car around her, closing windows, shrugging into her seat.

'Very pleasant, really. Nice chap.'

'I liked him. Not quite so sure about her.'

'It's pricey, of course.'

'All the same ...'

'Money well spent, though. One way and another.'

'Shall we settle it, then?'

'I think so. I'll drop him a line.'

The mother pitched her voice a notch higher to speak to the child in the back of the car. 'Would you like to go there, Charles? Like Simon Wilcox. Did you see that lovely gym, and the swimming-pool? And did the other boys tell you all about it?'

The child does not answer. He looks straight ahead of him, at the road coiling beneath the bonnet of the car. His face is haggard with anticipation.

Through the Tunnel

by Doris Lessing

Going to the shore on the first morning of the holiday, the young English boy stopped at a turning of the path and looked down at a wild and rocky bay, and then over to the crowded beach he knew so well from other years. His mother walked on in front of him, carrying a bright striped bag in one hand. Her other arm, swinging loose, was very white in the sun. The boy watched that white, naked arm, and turned his eyes, which had a frown behind them, towards the bay and back again to his mother. When she felt he was not with her, she swung around. 'Oh, there you are, Jerry!' she said. She looked impatient, then smiled. 'Why, darling, would you rather not come with me? Would you rather –' She frowned, conscientiously worrying over what amusements he might secretly be longing for, which she had been too busy or too careless to imagine. He was very familiar with that anxious, apologetic smile. Contrition[1] sent him running after her. And yet, as he ran, he looked back over his shoulder at the wild bay; and all morning, as he played on the safe beach, he was thinking of it.

Next morning, when it was time for the routine of swimming and sunbathing, his mother said, 'Are you tired of the usual beach, Jerry? Would you like to go somewhere else?'

[1] guilt

'Oh, no!' he said quickly, smiling at her out of that unfailing impulse of contrition – a sort of chivalry.[2] Yet, walking down the path with her, he blurted out, 'I'd like to go and have a look at those rocks down there.'

She gave the idea her attention. It was a wild-looking place, and there was no one there; but she said, 'Of course, Jerry. When you've had enough, come to the big beach. Or just go straight back to the villa, if you like.' She walked away, that bare arm, now slightly reddened from yesterday's sun, swinging. And he almost ran after her again, feeling it unbearable that she should go by herself, but he did not.

She was thinking, Of course he's old enough to be safe without me. Have I been keeping him too close? He mustn't feel he ought to be with me. I must be careful.

He was an only child, eleven years old. She was a widow. She was determined to be neither possessive nor lacking in devotion. She went worrying off to her beach.

As for Jerry, once he saw that his mother had gained her beach, he began the steep descent to the bay. From where he was, high up among red-brown rocks, it was a scoop of moving bluish green fringed with white. As he went lower, he saw that it spread among small promontories and inlets of rough, sharp rock, and the crisping, lapping surface showed stains of purple and darker blue. Finally, as he ran sliding and scraping down the last few yards, he saw an edge of white surf and the shallow, luminous movement of water over white sand, and, beyond that, a solid heavy blue.

He ran straight into the water and began swimming. He was a good swimmer. He went out fast over the

---

[2] courteous behaviour towards women

gleaming sand, over a middle region where rocks lay like discoloured monsters under the surface and then he was in the real sea – a warm sea where irregular cold currents from the deep water shocked his limbs.

When he was so far out that he could look back not only on the little bay but past the promontory that was between it and the big beach, he floated on the buoyant surface and looked for his mother. There she was, a speck of yellow under an umbrella that looked like a slice of orange peel. He swam back to shore, relieved at being sure she was there, but all at once very lonely.

On the edge of a small cape that marked the side of the bay away from the promontory was a loose scatter of rocks. Above them, some boys were stripping off their clothes. They came running, naked, down to the rocks. The English boy swam towards them, but kept his distance at a stone's throw. They were of that coast; all of them were burned smooth dark brown and speaking a language he did not understand. To be with them, of them, was a craving that filled his whole body. He swam a little closer; they turned and watched him with narrowed, alert dark eyes. Then one smiled and waved. It was enough. In a minute, he had swum in and was on the rocks beside them, smiling with a desperate, nervous supplication.[3] They shouted cheerful greetings at him; and then, as he preserved his nervous, uncomprehending smile, they understood that he was a foreigner strayed from his own beach, and they proceeded to forget him. But he was happy. He was with them.

They began diving again and again from a high point into a well of blue sea between rough, pointed rocks. After they had dived and come up, they swam around,

[3] trying hard to be liked

hauled themselves up, and waited their turn to dive again. They were big boys – men, to Jerry. He dived, and they watched him; and when he swam around to take his place, they made way for him. He felt he was accepted and he dived again, carefully, proud of himself.

Soon the biggest of the boys poised himself, shot down into the water, and did not come up. The others stood about, watching. Jerry, after waiting for the sleek brown head to appear, let out a yell of warning; they looked at him idly and turned their eyes back towards the water. After a long time, the boy came up on the other side of a big dark rock, letting the air out of his lungs in a sputtering gasp and a shout of triumph. Immediately the rest of them dived in. One moment, the morning seemed full of chattering boys; the next, the air and the surface of the water were empty. But through the heavy blue, dark shapes could be seen moving and groping.

Jerry dived, shot past the school of underwater swimmers, saw a black wall of rock looming at him, touched it, and bobbed up at once to the surface, where the wall was a low barrier he could see across. There was no one visible; under him, in the water, the dim shapes of the swimmers had disappeared. Then one, and then another of the boys came up on the far side of the barrier of rock, and he understood that they had swum through some gap or hole in it. He plunged down again. He could see nothing through the stinging salt water but the blank rock. When he came up the boys were all on the diving rock, preparing to attempt the feat again. And now, in a panic of failure, he yelled up, in English, 'Look at me! Look!' and he began splashing and kicking in the water like a foolish dog.

They looked down gravely, frowning. He knew the

frown. At moments of failure, when he clowned to claim his mother's attention, it was with just this grave, embarrassed inspection that she rewarded him. Through his hot shame, feeling the pleading grin on his face like a scar that he could never remove, he looked up at the group of big brown boys on the rock and shouted, '*Bonjour! Merci! Au revoir! Monsieur, monsieur!*' while he hooked his fingers round his ears and waggled them.

Water surged into his mouth; he choked, sank, came up. The rock, lately weighted with boys, seemed to rear up out of the water as their weight was removed. They were flying down past him now, into the water; the air was full of falling bodies. Then the rock was empty in the hot sunlight. He counted one, two, three . . .

At fifty, he was terrified. They must all be drowning beneath him, in the watery caves of the rock. At a hundred, he stared around him at the empty hillside, wondering if he should yell for help. He counted faster, faster, to hurry them up, to bring them to the surface quickly, to drown them quickly – anything rather than the terror of counting on and on into the blue emptiness of the morning. And then, at a hundred and sixty, the water beyond the rock was full of boys blowing like brown whales. They swam back to the shore without a look at him.

He climbed back to the diving rock and sat down, feeling the hot roughness of it under his thighs. The boys were gathering up their bits of clothing and running off along the shore to another promontory. They were leaving to get away from him. He cried openly, fists in his eyes. There was no one to see him, and he cried himself out.

It seemed to him that a long time had passed, and he swam out to where he could see his mother. Yes, she was

25

still there, a yellow spot under an orange umbrella. He swam back to the big rock, climbed up, and dived into the blue pool among the fanged and angry boulders. Down he went, until he touched the wall of rock again. But the salt was so painful in his eyes that he could not see.

He came to the surface, swam to shore and went back to the villa to wait for his mother. Soon she walked slowly up the path, swinging her striped bag, the flushed, naked arm dangling beside her. 'I want some swimming goggles,' he panted, defiant and beseeching.

She gave him a patient, inquisitive look as she said casually, 'Well, of course, darling.'

But now, now, now! He must have them this minute, and no other time. He nagged and pestered until she went with him to a shop. As soon as she had bought the goggles, he grabbed them from her hand as if she were going to claim them for herself, and was off, running down the steep path to the bay.

Jerry swam out to the big barrier rock, adjusted the goggles, and dived. The impact of the water broke the rubber-enclosed vacuum, and the goggles came loose. He understood that he must swim down to the base of the rock from the surface of the water. He fixed the goggles tight and firm, filled his lungs, and floated, face down, on the water. Now, he could see. It was as if he had eyes of a different kind – fish eyes that showed everything clear and delicate and wavering in the bright water.

Under him, six or seven feet down, was a floor of perfectly clean, shining white sand, rippled firm and hard by the tides. Two greyish shapes steered there, like long, rounded pieces of wood or slate. They were fish. He saw them nose towards each other, poise motionless, make a dart forward, swerve off, and come around again. It was like a water dance. A few inches above them the water sparkled as if sequins were dropping through it. Fish again – myriads of minute fish, the length of his fingernail, were drifting through the water, and in a moment he could feel the innumerable tiny touches of them against his limbs. It was like swimming in flaked silver. The great rock the big boys had swum through rose sheer out of the white sand – black, tufted lightly with greenish weed. He could see no gap in it. He swam down to its base.

Again and again he rose, took a big chestful of air, and went down again. Again and again he groped over the surface of the rock, feeling it, almost hugging it in the desperate need to find the entrance. And then, once, while he was clinging to the black wall, his knees came up and he shot his feet out forward and they met no obstacle. He had found the hole.

He gained the surface, clambered about the stones that littered the barrier rock until he found a big one, and, with this in his arms, let himself down over the side of the rock. He dropped, with the weight, straight to the sandy floor. Clinging tight to the anchor of stone, he lay on his side and looked in under the dark shelf at the place where his feet had gone. He could see the hole. It was an irregular, dark gap but he could not see deep into it. He let go of his anchor, clung with his hands to the edges of the hole, and tried to push himself in.

He got his head in, found his shoulders jammed, moved them in sideways, and was inside as far as his waist. He could see nothing ahead. Something soft and clammy touched his mouth; he saw a dark frond moving against the greyish rock, and panic filled him. He thought of octopuses, of clinging weed. He pushed himself out backwards and caught a glimpse, as he retreated, of a harmless tentacle of seaweed drifting in the mouth of the tunnel. But it was enough. He reached the sunlight, swam to shore, and lay on the diving rock. He looked down into the blue well of water. He knew he must find his way through that cave, or hole, or tunnel, and out the other side.

First, he thought, he must learn to control his breathing. He let himself down into the water with another big stone in his arms, so that he could lie effortlessly on the bottom of the sea. He counted. One, two, three. He counted steadily. He could hear the movement of blood in his chest. Fifty-one, fifty-two ... His chest was hurting. He let go of the rock and went up into the air. He saw the sun was low. He rushed to the villa and found his mother at her supper. She said only, 'Did you enjoy yourself?' and he said, 'Yes.'

All night the boy dreamed of the water-filled cave in the rock, and as soon as breakfast was over he went to the bay.

That night, his nose bled badly. For hours he had been underwater, learning to hold his breath, and now he felt weak and dizzy. His mother said, 'I shouldn't overdo things, darling, if I were you.'

That day and the next, Jerry exercised his lungs as if everything, the whole of his life, all that he would become, depended upon it. Again his nose bled at night, and his mother insisted on his coming with her the next day. It was a torment to him to waste a day of his careful self-training, but he stayed with her on that other beach, which now seemed a place for small children, a place where his mother might lie safe in the sun. It was not his beach.

He did not ask for permission, on the following day, to go to his beach. He went, before his mother could consider the complicated rights and wrongs of the matter. A day's rest, he discovered, had improved his count by ten. The big boys had made the passage while he counted a hundred and sixty. He had been counting fast, in his fright. Probably now, if he tried, he could get through that long tunnel, but he was not going to try yet. A curious, most unchildlike persistence, a controlled impatience, made him wait. In the meantime, he lay underwater on the white sand, littered now by stones he had brought down from the upper air, and studied the entrance to the tunnel. He knew every jut and corner of it, as far as it was possible to see. It was as if he already felt its sharpness about his shoulders.

He sat by the clock in the villa, when his mother was not near, and checked his time. He was incredulous and then proud to find he could hold his breath without strain for two minutes. The words, 'two minutes,' authorised by the clock, brought close the adventure that was so necessary to him.

In another four days, his mother said casually one morning, they must go home. On the day before they left, he would do it. He would do it if it killed him, he said defiantly to himself. But two days before they were to leave – a day of triumph when he increased his count by fifteen – his nose bled so badly that he turned dizzy and had to lie limply over the big rock like a bit of seaweed, watching the thick red blood flow on to the rock and trickle slowly down to the sea. He was frightened. Supposing he turned dizzy in the tunnel? Supposing he died there, trapped? Supposing – his head went around, in the hot sun, and he almost gave up. He thought he would return to the house and lie down, and next summer, perhaps when he had another year's growth in him – *then* he would go through the hole.

But even after he had made the decision, or thought he had, he found himself sitting up on the rock and looking down into the water; and he knew that now, this moment, when his nose had only just stopped bleeding, when his head was still sore and throbbing – this was the moment when he would try. If he did not do it now, he never would. He was trembling with fear that he would not go; and he was trembling with horror at that long, long tunnel under the rock, under the sea. Even in the open sunlight, the barrier rock seemed very wide and very heavy; tons of rock pressed down on where he would go. If he died there, he would lie until one day – perhaps not before next year – those big boys would swim into it and find it blocked.

He put on his goggles, fitted them tight, tested the vacuum. His hands were shaking. Then he chose the biggest stone he could carry and slipped over the edge of the rock until half of him was in the cool, enclosing water and half in the hot sun. He looked up once at the empty sky, filled his lungs once, twice, and then sank fast to the bottom with the stone. He let it go and began to count. He took the edges of the hole in his hands and drew himself into it, wriggling his shoulders in sideways as he remembered he must, kicking himself along with his feet.

Soon he was clear inside. He was in a small rock-bound hole filled with yellowish-grey water. The water was pushing him up against the roof. The roof was sharp and pained his back. He pulled himself along with his hands – fast, fast – and used his legs as levers. His head knocked against something; a sharp pain dizzied him. Fifty, fifty-one, fifty-two ... He was without light, and the water seemed to press upon him with the weight of rock. Seventy-one, seventy-two ... There was no strain on his lungs. He felt like an inflated balloon, his lungs were so light and easy, but his head was pulsing.

He was being continually pressed against the sharp roof, which felt slimy as well as sharp. Again he thought of octopuses, and wondered if the tunnel might be filled with weed that could tangle him. He gave himself a panicky, convulsive kick forward, ducked his head, and swam. His feet and hands moved freely, as if in open water. The hole must have widened out. He thought he must be swimming fast, and he was frightened of banging his head if the tunnel narrowed.

A hundred, a hundred and one ... The water paled. Victory filled him. His lungs were beginning to hurt. A few more strokes and he would be out. He was counting wildly; he said a hundred and fifteen, and then, a long time later, a hundred and fifteen again. The water was a clear jewel-green all around him. Then he saw, above his head, a crack running up through the rock. Sunlight was falling through it, showing the clean, dark rock of the tunnel, a single mussel shell, and darkness ahead.

He was at the end of what he could do. He looked up at the crack as if it were filled with air and not water, as if he could put his mouth to it and draw air. A hundred and fifteen, he heard himself say inside his head – but he had said that long ago. He must go on into the blackness ahead, or he would drown. His head was swelling, his lungs cracking. A hundred and fifteen, a hundred and fifteen pounded through his head, and he feebly clutched at rocks in the dark, pulling himself forward, leaving the brief space of sunlit water behind. He felt he was dying. He was no longer quite conscious. He struggled on in the darkness between lapses into unconsciousness. An immense, swelling pain filled his head, and then the darkness cracked with an explosion of green light. His hands, groping forward, met nothing; and his feet, kicking back, propelled him out into the open sea.

He drifted to the surface, his face turned up to the air. He was gasping like a fish. He felt he would sink now and drown; he could not swim the few feet back to the rock. Then he was clutching it and pulling himself up on to it. He lay face down, gasping. He could see nothing but a red-veined, clotted dark. His eyes must have burst, he thought; they were full of blood. He tore off his goggles and a gout of blood went into the sea. His nose was bleeding, and the blood had filled the goggles.

He scooped up handfuls of water from the cool, salty sea, to splash on his face, and did not know whether it was blood or salt water he tasted. After a time, his heart quietened, his eyes cleared, and he sat up. He could see the local boys diving and playing half a mile away. He did not want them. He wanted nothing but to get back home and lie down.

In a short while, Jerry swam to the shore and climbed slowly up the path to the villa. He flung himself on his bed and slept, waking at the sound of feet on the path outside. His mother was coming back. He rushed to the bathroom, thinking she must not see his face with bloodstains, or tearstains, on it. He came out of the bathroom and met her as she walked into the villa, smiling, her eyes lighting up.

'Have a nice morning?' she asked, laying her hand on his warm brown shoulder a moment.

'Oh yes, thank you,' he said.

'You look a bit pale.' And then, sharp and anxious, 'How did you bang your head?'

'Oh, just banged it,' he told her.

She looked at him closely. He was strained; his eyes were glazed-looking. She was worried. And then she said to herself, Oh, don't fuss! Nothing can happen. He can swim like a fish.

They sat down to lunch together.

'Mummy,' he said, 'I can stay under water for two minutes – three minutes, at least.' It came bursting out of him.

'Can you, darling?' she said. 'Well, I shouldn't overdo it. I don't think you ought to swim any more today.'

She was ready for a battle of wills, but he gave in at once. It was no longer of the least importance to go to the bay.

The Voyage

by Katherine Mansfield

The Picton boat was due to leave at half past eleven. It was a beautiful night, mild, starry, only when they got out of the cab and started to walk down the Old Wharf that jutted out into the harbour, a faint wind blowing off the water ruffled under Fenella's hat, and she put up her hand to keep it on. It was dark on the Old Wharf, very dark; the wool sheds, the cattle trucks, the cranes standing up so high, the little squat railway engine, all seemed carved out of solid darkness. Here and there on a rounded wood-pile, that was like the stalk of a huge black mushroom, there hung a lantern, but it seemed afraid to unfurl its timid, quivering light in all that blackness; it burned softly, as if for itself.

Fenella's father pushed on with quick, nervous strides. Beside him her grandma bustled along in her crackling black ulster;[1] they went so fast that she had now and again to give an undignified little skip to keep up with them. As well as her luggage strapped into a neat sausage, Fenella carried clasped to her her grandma's umbrella, and the handle, which was a swan's head, kept giving her shoulder a sharp little peck as if it too wanted her to hurry ... Men, their caps pulled down, their collars turned up, swung by; a few women all muffled scurried along; and one tiny boy, only his little black arms and legs showing out of a white

[1] heavy coat

woolly shawl, was jerked along angrily between his father and mother; he looked like a baby fly that had fallen into the cream.

Then suddenly, so suddenly that Fenella and her grandma both leapt, there sounded from behind the largest wool shed, that had a trail of smoke hanging over it, *Mia-oo-oo-O-O*!

'First whistle,' said her father briefly, and at that moment they came in sight of the Picton boat. Lying beside the dark wharf, all strung, all beaded with round golden lights, the Picton boat looked as if she was more ready to sail among stars than out into the cold sea. People pressed along the gangway. First went her grandma, then her father, then Fenella. There was a high step down on to the deck, and an old sailor in a jersey standing by gave her his dry, hard hand. They were there; they stepped out of the way of the hurrying people, and standing under a little iron stairway that led to the upper deck they began to say good-bye.

'There, mother, there's your luggage!' said Fenella's father, giving Grandma another strapped-up sausage.

'Thank you, Frank.'

'And you've got your cabin tickets safe?'

'Yes, dear.'

'And your other tickets?'

Grandma felt for them inside her glove and showed him the tips.

'That's right.'

He sounded stern, but Fenella, eagerly watching him, saw that he looked tired and sad. *Mia-oo-oo-O-O*! The second whistle blared just above their heads, and a voice like a cry shouted, 'Any more for the gangway?'

'You'll give my love to Father,' Fenella saw her father's lips say. And her grandma, very agitated, answered, 'Of course I will, dear. Go now. You'll be left. Go now, Frank. Go now.'

'It's all right, Mother. I've got another three minutes.' To her surprise Fenella saw her father take off his hat. He clasped Grandma in his arms and pressed her to him. 'God bless you, Mother!' she heard him say.

And Grandma put her hand, with the black thread glove that was worn through on her ring finger, against his cheek, and she sobbed, 'God bless you, my own brave son!'

This was so awful that Fenella quickly turned her back on them, swallowed once, twice, and frowned terribly at a little green star on a mast head. But she had to turn round again; her father was going.

'Good-bye, Fenella. Be a good girl.' His cold wet moustache brushed her cheek. But Fenella caught hold of the lapels of his coat.

'How long am I going to stay?' she whispered anxiously. He wouldn't look at her. He shook her off gently, and gently said, 'We'll see about that. Here! Where's your hand?' He pressed something into her palm. 'Here's a shilling in case you should need it.'

A shilling! She must be going away for ever! 'Father!' cried Fenella. But he was gone. He was the last off the ship. The sailors put their shoulders to the gangway. A huge coil of dark rope went flying through the air and fell 'thump' on the wharf. A bell rang; a whistle shrilled. Silently the dark wharf began to slip, to slide, to edge away from them. Now there was a rush of water between. Fenella strained to see with all her might. 'Was that Father turning round?' – or waving? – or standing alone? – or walking off by himself? The strip of water grew broader, darker. Now the Picton boat began to swing round steady, pointing out to sea. It was no good looking any longer. There was nothing to be seen but a few lights, the face of the town clock hanging in the air, and more lights, little patches of them, on the dark hills.

The freshening wind tugged at Fenella's skirts; she went back to her grandma. To her relief Grandma seemed no longer sad. She had put the two sausages of luggage one on top of the other, and she was sitting on them, her hands folded, her head a little on one side. There was an intent, bright look on her face. Then Fenella saw that her lips were moving and guessed that she was praying. But the old woman gave her a bright nod as if to say the prayer was nearly over. She unclasped her hands, sighed, clasped them again, bent forward, and at last gave herself a soft shake.

'And now, child,' she said, fingering the bow of her bonnet-strings, 'I think we ought to see about our cabins. Keep close to me, and mind you don't slip.'

'Yes, Grandma!'

'And be careful the umbrellas aren't caught in the stair rail. I saw a beautiful umbrella broken in half like that on my way over.'

'Yes, Grandma.'

Dark figures of men lounged against the rails. In the glow of their pipes a nose shone out, or the peak of a cap, or a pair of surprised-looking eyebrows. Fenella glanced up. High in the air, a little figure, his hand thrust in his short jacket pockets, stood staring out to sea. The ship rocked ever so little, and she thought the stars rocked too. And now a pale steward in a linen coat, holding a tray high in the palm of his hand, stepped out of a lighted doorway and skimmed past them. They went through that doorway. Carefully over the high brass-bound step on to the rubber mat and then down such a terribly steep flight of stairs that Grandma had to put both feet on each step, and Fenella clutched the clammy brass rail and forgot all about the swan-necked umbrella.

At the bottom Grandma stopped; Fenella was rather afraid she was going to pray again. But no, it was only to get out the cabin tickets. They were in the saloon. It was glaring bright and stifling; the air smelled of paint and burnt chop-bones and india-rubber. Fenella wished her grandma would go on, but the old woman was not to be hurried. An immense basket of ham sandwiches caught her eye. She went up to them and touched the top one delicately with her finger.

'How much are the sandwiches?' she asked.

'Tuppence!' bawled a rude steward, slamming down a knife and fork.

Grandma could hardly believe it.

'Two pence *each*?' she asked.

'That's right,' said the steward, and he winked at his companion.

Grandma made a small, astonished face. Then she whispered primly to Fenella. 'What wickedness!' And they sailed out at the further door and along a passage that had cabins on either side. Such a very nice stewardess came to meet them. She was dressed all in blue, and her collar and cuffs were fastened with large brass buttons. She seemed to know Grandma well.

'Well, Mrs Crane,' said she, unlocking their wash-stand. 'We've got you back again. It's not often you give yourself a cabin.'

'No,' said Grandma. 'But this time my dear son's thoughtfulness –'

'I hope –' began the stewardess. Then she turned round and took a long mournful look at Grandma's blackness and at Fenella's black coat and skirt, black blouse, and hat with a crape rose.

Grandma nodded. 'It was God's will,' said she.

The stewardess shut her lips and, taking a deep breath, she seemed to expand.

'What I always say is,' she said, as though it was her own discovery, 'sooner or later each of us has to go, and that's a certingty.' She paused. 'Now, can I bring you anything, Mrs Crane? A cup of tea? I know it's no good offering you a little something to keep the cold out.'

Grandma shook her head. 'Nothing, thank you. We've got a few wine biscuits, and Fenella has a very nice banana.'

'Then I'll give you a look later on,' said the stewardess, and she went out, shutting the door.

What a very small cabin it was! It was like being shut up in a box with Grandma. The dark round eye above the washstand gleamed at them dully. Fenella felt shy. She stood against the door, still clasping her luggage and the umbrella. Were they going to get undressed in here? Already her grandma had taken off her bonnet, and, rolling up the strings, she fixed each with a pin to the lining before she hung the bonnet up. Her white hair shone like silk; the little bun at the back was covered with a black net. Fenella hardly ever saw her grandma with her head uncovered; she looked strange.

'I shall put on the woollen fascinator[2] your dear mother crocheted for me,' said Grandma, and, unstrapping the sausage, she took it out and wound it round her head; the fringe of grey bobbles danced at her eyebrows as she smiled tenderly and mournfully at Fenella. Then she undid her bodice, and something under that, and something else underneath that. Then there seemed a short, sharp tussle, and Grandma flushed faintly. Snip! Snap! She had undone her stays. She breathed a sigh of relief, and sitting on the plush

[2] woollen head-covering for women

couch, she slowly and carefully pulled off her elastic-sided boots and stood them side by side.

By the time Fenella had taken off her coat and skirt and put on her flannel dressing-gown Grandma was quite ready.

'Must I take off my boots, Grandma? They're lace.'

Grandma gave them a moment's deep consideration. 'You'd feel a great deal more comfortable if you did, child,' said she. She kissed Fenella. 'Don't forget to say your prayers. Our dear Lord is with us when we are at sea even more than when we are on dry land. And because I am an experienced traveller,' said Grandma briskly, 'I shall take the upper berth.'

'But, Grandma, however will you get up there?'

Three little spider-like steps were all Fenella saw. The old woman gave a small silent laugh before she mounted them nimbly, and she peered over the high bunk at the astonished Fenella.

'You didn't think your grandma could do that, did you?' said she. And as she sank back Fenella heard her light laugh again.

The hard square of brown soap would not lather, and the water in the bottle was like a kind of blue jelly. How hard it was, too, to turn down those stiff sheets; you simply had to tear your way in. If everything had been different, Fenella might have got the giggles ... At last she was inside, and while she lay there panting, there sounded from above a long, soft whispering, as though someone was gently, gently rustling among tissue paper to find something. It was Grandma saying her prayers ...

A long time passed. Then the stewardess came in; she trod softly and leaned her hand on Grandma's bunk.

'We're just entering the Straits,' she said.

'Oh!'

'It's a fine night, but we're rather empty. We may pitch a little.'

And indeed at that moment the Picton boat rose and rose and hung in the air just long enough to give a shiver before she swung down again, and there was the sound of heavy water slapping against her sides. Fenella remembered she had left that swan-necked umbrella standing up on the little couch. If it fell over, would it break? But Grandma remembered too, at the same time.

'I wonder if you'd mind, stewardess, laying down my umbrella,' she whispered.

'Not at all, Mrs Crane.' And the stewardess, coming back to Grandma, breathed, 'Your little grand-daughter's in such a beautiful sleep.'

'God be praised for that!' said Grandma.

'Poor little motherless mite!' said the stewardess. And Grandma was still telling the stewardess all about what happened when Fenella fell asleep.

But she hadn't been asleep long enough to dream before she woke up again to see something waving in the air above her head. What was it? What could it be? It was a small grey foot. Now another joined it. They seemed to be feeling about for something; there came a sigh.

'I'm awake, Grandma,' said Fenella.

'Oh, dear, am I near the ladder?' asked Grandma. 'I thought it was this end.'

'No, Grandma, it's the other. I'll put your foot on it. Are we there?' asked Fenella.

'In the harbour,' said Grandma. 'We must get up, child. You'd better have a biscuit to steady yourself before you move.'

But Fenella had hopped out of her bunk. The lamp was still burning, but night was over, and it was cold.

Peering through that round eye, she could see far off some rocks. Now they were scattered over with foam; now a gull flipped by; and now there came a long piece of real land.

'It's land, Grandma,' said Fenella, wonderingly, as though they had been at sea for weeks together. She hugged herself; she stood on one leg and rubbed it with the toes of the other foot; she was trembling. Oh, it had all been so sad lately. Was it going to change? But all her Grandma said was, 'Make haste, child. I should leave your nice banana for the stewardess as you haven't eaten it.' And Fenella put on her black clothes again, and a button sprang off one of her gloves and rolled to where she couldn't reach it. They went up on deck.

But if it had been cold in the cabin, on deck it was like ice. The sun was not up yet, but the stars were dim, and the cold pale sky was the same colour as the cold pale sea. On the land a white mist rose and fell. Now they could see quite plainly dark bush. Even the shapes of the umbrella ferns showed, and those strange silvery withered trees that are like skeletons ... Now they could see the landing-stage and some little houses, pale too, clustered together, like shells on the lid of a box. The other passengers tramped up and down, but more slowly than they had the night before, and they looked gloomy.

And now the landing-stage came out to meet them. Slowly it swam towards the Picton boat, and a man holding a coil of rope, and a cart with a small drooping horse and another man sitting on the step, came too.

'It's Mr Penreddy, Fenella, come for us,' said Grandma. She sounded pleased. Her white waxen cheeks were blue with cold, her chin trembled, and she had to keep wiping her eyes and her little pink nose.

'You've got my –'

'Yes, Grandma.' Fenella showed it to her.

The rope came flying through the air, and 'smack' it fell on to the deck. The gangway was lowered. Again Fenella followed her grandma on to the wharf over to the little cart, and a moment later they were bowling away. The hooves of the little horse drummed over the wooden piles, then sank softly into the sandy road. Not a soul was to be seen; there was not even a feather of smoke. The mist rose and fell, and the sea still sounded asleep as slowly it turned on the beach.

'I seen Mr Crane yestiddy,' said Mr Penreddy. 'He looked himself then. Missus knocked him up a batch of scones last week.'

And now the little horse pulled up before one of the shell-like houses. They got down. Fenella put her hand on the gate, and the big, trembling dewdrops soaked through her glove-tips. Up a little path of round white pebbles they went, with drenched sleeping flowers on either side. Grandma's delicate white picotees[3] were so heavy with dew that they were fallen, but their sweet smell was part of the cold morning. The blinds were down in the little house; they mounted the steps on to the veranda. A pair of old bluchers was on one side of the door, and a large red water-can on the other.

'Tut! tut! Your grandpa,' said Grandma. She turned the handle. Not a sound. She called, 'Walter!' And immediately a deep voice that sounded half stifled called back, 'Is that you, Mary?'

'Wait, dear,' said Grandma. 'Go in there.' She pushed Fenella gently into a small dusky sitting-room.

On the table a white cat, that had been folded up like a camel, rose, stretched itself, yawned, and then sprang on to the tips of its toes. Fenella buried one cold little

[3] carnations whose pale petals are tinged with darker-coloured edges

hand in the white, warm fur, and smiled timidly while she stroked and listened to Grandma's gentle voice and the rolling tones of Grandpa.

A door creaked. 'Come in, dear.' The old woman beckoned, Fenella followed. There, lying to one side of an immense bed, lay Grandpa. Just his head with a white tuft, and his rosy face and long silver beard showed over the quilt. He was like a very old wide-awake bird.

'Well, my girl!' said Grandpa. 'Give us a kiss!' Fenella kissed him. 'Ugh!' said Grandpa. 'Her little nose is as cold as a button. What's that she's holding? Her grandma's umbrella?'

Fenella smiled again, and crooked the swan neck over the bed-rail. Above the bed there was a big text in a deep-black frame:

> Lost! One Golden Hour
> Set with Sixty Diamond Minutes.
> No Reward Is Offered
> For It Is GONE FOR EVER!

'Yer grandma painted that,' said Grandpa. And he ruffled his white tuft and looked at Fenella so merrily she almost thought he winked at her.

The Elephant Man

by Susan Hill

It was on the same day that they drained the Round Pond, for the first time in forty years, that Nanny Fawcett met her Friend. And in all the time the three of them spent together afterwards, she never gave him any name in front of the child, he was always My Friend.

William had asked anxiously about the Pond, what it would look like, how big it would be now?

'The same size as always, won't it? *That's* a silly question.'

'Just with no water in it?'

'We don't say "with no" we say "without any".'

'Yes. How big will the pit be?'

'What pit? There won't be any *pit*, will there? Lift your arms up.'

The stream of lather came trickling around both sides of his neck and down his pale chest. At the edges of the bath, the scum was grey, when the water moved. He struggled to imagine the Round Pond, to which he went every day, empty of its expanse of water, rippled across the centre by the wind, but he failed, he could not picture it and was alarmed by his ignorance of how it might be.

'If there won't be a pit, what *will* there be, then?'

A grip fell down into the bath out of Nanny Fawcett's coiled-up red hair, as she bent over him.

'Mud,' she said sharply. 'Stand up.' There was a line of sweat-beads along her upper lip. She retrieved the grip

45

impatiently. Wary of her moods, which came unpre-
dictably, and then hung about her, thickening and
tainting the atmosphere of rooms, he did not ask what
would have happened to the ducks. He imagined them,
kept in individual, waterless cages, and fed by keepers
with broken bread, and later, hung in rows by their
webbed, pink feet along the steel rail at Murchison's,
Butcher and Poulterer.

Nanny Fawcett began to rub him with a very dry
towel.

At the beginning, there had been another Nanny,
about whom he now remembered only a smell, and an
air of weariness and loss of hope. 'I was trained in the
old school,' she had said, on arrival, 'I am only used to
the best type of home.' And she had been firm in her
demands for Sole Charge and no sweets of any kind
and the sacking of the cleaning woman who used bad
language. 'But then she is so reliable and decided,'
William's mother had said, sipping a Manhattan[1] in the
oyster-grey drawing-room, 'everything is so nice for me,
so straightforward.' Though, in truth, she felt a little
guilty that this was so, believed obscurely that it was not
altogether natural to have a nanny who gave simply no
trouble. So that it had been almost a salve to her
conscience when that Nanny had, abruptly, died, and
the problems of finding someone new and suitable
began. William was three and a half.

He could not now imagine how it had been before
Nanny Fawcett came to the house, he saw the world
entirely through her eyes, all his experience of life
reached him filtered through her. Nanny Fawcett was
Irish, she was in her middle thirties, she came from a
good, Protestant family in Dublin, she was moody. Her

[1] a cocktail

breasts were too large and concealed a heart filled with prejudice, most markedly against men, and against the Republic of Eire.

William's mother had some weeks of anxiety. 'I do hope we have done the right thing, she did *seem* the most suitable, though it is clear to us all that Nannies are not what they were. But I am afraid that I suspect Nanny Fawcett of dying her hair. That red is so unnatural.' She spoke as one of some distant generation, but she was not old-fashioned, merely true to her breeding. She spoke in a high-pitched, nasal, slightly whining voice. But she felt, too, a little more comfortable with Nanny Fawcett, felt secure in her own position as mistress of both house and child. It was only what one expected, to have to put up with some quirks, in a Nanny.

When they visited the house in Cadogan Square, William's maternal grandmother sat among the fringed sofas from Peter Jones,[2] the skin beneath her eyes most carefully powdered, and asked, 'What about this Nanny Fawcett?' 'But I think, you know,' said William's mother, when they had discussed it, 'that she is *all right*, I think that everything is as it should be, on the whole. Of course, I would never entrust William to just anybody.'

They could feel their duty done, then, and dismiss the child's welfare under Nanny Fawcett from their minds.

To William, the only realities of which he could be certain, the only truths he knew, came to him through Nanny Fawcett. Everywhere else was the territory of strangers, the ground upon which he walked, in company with his mother and father and the Cadogan

[2] a department store in London

Square grandmother, was insubstantial. He sensed that he could never have survived, permanently, in their atmosphere. From Nanny Fawcett he learned that there were 'Irish *and* Irish,' and that the Protestants of good family living in Dublin kept themselves very much to themselves, they had their own clubs and dances and private schools.

'A trained Nanny,' she said, over and over again, 'is not a servant. This is a profession. I am not a *maid*, you know, nothing of that kind.'

He learned about the spoliation of Dublin's Georgian buildings and about the low character of the feckless Southern Irish, Roman Catholic and working class, who came over to England and gave their country a bad name. He learned about the winning ways and loose morals of the colleens[3] who worked as waitresses in Lyons Corner House and conductresses on buses of the Green Line. He learned about the integrity of the Unionist party and the reign of terror by bigoted priests among the peasants of Eire. He learned that Nanny Fawcett's grandmother bred Irish setter dogs, and that her family had always been 'proud'. Above all, he learned that most of the trouble in the world, and all the troubles of women, could be laid at the door of men.

'You'll be a man,' she said, laying his checked Viyella shirt out on the chair. 'You'll be as bad as all the rest.' And he had felt suddenly ashamed, knowing that his days were strictly numbered with her. He wished that he might do something to change his sex, to grow up or in some other way escape from the general mantle of male guilt. He was uncertain how he stood with Nanny Fawcett, what she truly thought of him. Her eyes,

[3] girls (from an Irish word)

upturned slightly at the corners like those of an Oriental, flitted over him and gave him no reassurance, nothing more than a casual, spasmodic approval for some point of manners remembered or temptation not succumbed to.[4] He planned ways to ingratiate himself[5] with her, so that he might perceive some definite sign that her commendation would last for ever. But always, the eyes swept quickly over him, and he despaired. There was only the immediate chance of an hour, or day, of favour to cling to, he learned to live his life in these small snatches. They were like stepping stones, below which ran the dark river of her moods.

And so, he was surprised, the first day they met the Friend. It was January, slate-grey, a cold wind cutting across between the trees at their legs. He began to trail behind Nanny Fawcett up the slope, anxious about how the Round Pond would look, of how he might cope with getting to know it all over again, the unfamiliar.

'Don't scrape your shoes, you've only just this week had a new pair.'

Today, her hair shone redder than before, and the coils were more elaborate, gripped under the navy-blue hat. She had said, 'You're to behave yourself very nicely and not to be a nuisance, you're to make a good impression.'

'Why?'

'Because we might be going to meet someone, that's why. And you're having a jumper on under that coat, the wind's enough to cut you in half.'

He wondered who it was that they might see, if it was not the other Nannies, beside whom she would some-times sit, on the green bench. Though, more often than

[4] given in to
[5] make himself liked

not, she ignored them, neither sat nor talked, preferring to keep herself apart. The others, she had told him, had nothing of interest to say, or else they gave themselves airs, or were in charge of unsuitable children.

'Who might we see?'

'Never you mind, you'll find out in good time – and that's something else, you're to be quiet and not to go pestering with questions like you do, and "I want this, I want that", every five minutes. *We* want a bit of peace and quiet to ourselves, my friend and I.'

He gave up trying to imagine what kind of friend Nanny Fawcett might have. At the top of the slope, he walked forwards a little, and then stopped. The Pond was huge, it had spread and spread, with the exit of the water it seemed to him that he would never be able to walk as far as the opposite edge, he could barely see it. It was mud, thick and stiff and sculptured into lines of thin waves, towards the rim, as though the water had coagulated. He noticed the boats, beached on the mud and larded with it, so that their shape was disguised. They had been there for years, he thought, since before he was born, they had been there for ever.

'Don't stand staring at that, it's only a basinful of mud, and thick with germs, I shouldn't wonder, there's nothing to see.'

But he could not take his eyes off the landscape of the pond, the craters and pits, the branches of trees and the abandoned boats picked out on it, he wanted to step down and walk across, poking and digging, to get into the centre where no one could reach him, not even the men with long grappling hooks, who sometimes had to bring the boats in, when the wind dropped.

Nanny Fawcett caught his hand. 'Did you *hear* me?' He went after her, away from the Pond and up towards the bandstand on the edge of the trees.

For a long time, nobody came. He went away from her and down between the horse-chestnut trees, mashing the old leaves with his feet. He found an almost straight stick and held it like a lance. No other children were here, only, some yards away, a woman in green with a dog. From the beginning the afternoon had been strangely different, this place was not like the gardens to which he usually came, to rush about and sail a boat, while Nanny Fawcett looked on. The whole landscape was changed, everything was coloured differently, and the trees were a new shape. The Pond was dry. They might have been in another country. He was excited by it, and a little alarmed.

From far away, down the pleached walk came the shouts of boys, high and thin in the wind. He began to poke about in the leaves again with his straight stick.

When he looked up, he saw that Nanny Fawcett's friend had arrived, they were sitting together beside the empty bandstand. Nanny Fawcett touched her hand now and again to the coils of hair underneath the navy-blue hat. After a moment or two, William went nearer. The·fact that her friend was a man completed his sense of strangeness, everything was suddenly out of joint in his view of the world and of people, if Nanny Fawcett, who despised men, could be so publicly friendly with one, nodding and smiling on the green bench.

He looked, William thought, as though his clothes did not belong to him, as though he were used to wearing something quite different. Though they were ordinary, a grey tweed overcoat, rather long, over grey trousers, and an egg-yellow scarf. And his face, the shape of his head and the set of his flesh across the bones, seemed not to fit with the rest of him, he was like a figure out of the Crazy Men game, where you moved a row of heads along, fitting them in turn to a row of different bodies underneath, and none of them seemed exactly to belong. Something in the man's features was constantly changing, as though he were trying on new expressions, toying with them and then discarding them, he smiled and grimaced and frowned and formed his mouth into a little, soft, pursed shape, and the flesh of his forehead slipped up and down somehow, under the shelf of thinning hair, the skin of his neck was loose.

William thought that he was old – and then not so old, it was hard to tell. He had a lot of very long teeth, and a tiny chin, and very pale, gloveless hands.

He moved the stick about on the grass at his feet, and Nanny Fawcett saw him.

'Come here now, you're not to go off too far into those trees by yourself – come right here. This is him, this is William – stand up properly, child – Now, *here* is the person I told you we might be going to meet.' She was talking much faster than usual, and every now and then, her hand went up to the coils of hair. William took a step nearer the bench, and the man leaned down and put out one of the pale hands, smiling with all his teeth, as though it were a joke, that they should be so formally introduced. William thought, he is not a very old man, but he is older than my father. He said, 'They've emptied the water out of the Round Pond. It's just mud now.'

'Ah!' said Nanny Fawcett's friend, and the expression on his face slipped and changed again, and now he looked secretive, he put a tongue inside his cheek and made it swell out a little, as though he were sucking a toffee. 'I daresay you wanted to sail a boat, didn't you? I daresay that's the trouble.'

'No, I didn't, I like it empty. I want it to stay like that.

There are boats that have sunk, you can see them. And twigs. There are ...'

'Off you go,' Nanny Fawcett said, suddenly impatient. 'Don't chatter so, about nothing, off you go and run about and don't wander too far off into those trees, do you hear me?'

He saw her turn a little on the bench, so that she was facing the Friend, saw a bright expression come into her face, as though everything he had said and would say were all that could interest her. The man turned his back, so that there was only the dark grey tweed and the line of yellow scarf below.

William moved away, chilled by the abrupt loss of their attention, and wandered about on the path by the trees. His hands were cold inside the woollen gloves. He wanted something to happen, for the day to become familiar again. Above his head, and stretching away into the distance, the sky was uniformly pale, and grey as brains. The woman in green, with the dog, had gone, everybody was going, out of the January wind.

Under one of the horse-chestnuts he found a conker, and although the green pulpy case had blemished, and the spines were soft and rotten, inside the nut was perfect, hard and polished like a mahogany table. He scooped it out and held it, feeling it slip, shiny, between his fingers. When he disturbed the leaves, the soil and moss beneath the trees sent up a cold, sweet stench.

He heard nothing, only saw the feet and legs in front of him. Very slowly he straightened up, holding the stick. It was another man. William glanced over to Nanny Fawcett, sitting with her friend on the park bench, wanting reassurance. Their faces were turned away from him.

'Nice,' the man said, 'that's nice.' His eyes were sharp

and vacant at the same time, and he had a tall head. William stepped back.

'I could give you another. I could give you a lot.' And suddenly his hand shot out from under the mackintosh, and in the open palm lay eight or nine conkers, huge and glossy. 'I might give them all to you.'

'That's all right, I've got my own, thank you,' William was afraid of not being polite enough to the man, touched by the offer of the conkers, yet uneasy, not liking him to be there. When he looked again, the conkers had disappeared, and so had the man's hand, back into the pocket of the raincoat, so that he wondered whether he had seen them or not, and the man stood, smiling at him. The collar of his shirt was stiff, and shiny white.

'What's your name?'

'William.'

'That's nice. That's what I like.'

A gust of wind came knifing through the trees, stirring the dead leaves, and rattling down a loose branch. Abruptly, the man turned and began to move away, slipping round the grey trunks until he had vanished as quickly as the conkers had vanished. William stood, remembering the way he had come there. He dropped the conker into his coat pocket and kept his fingers tightly round it.

'Men,' Nanny Fawcett had said. 'There's always something that's not right about men, always something.' Now, he felt betrayed somehow, left alone among the trees with a stranger who offered him conkers, while she went on talking to her new friend.

On the way home, he asked if they would see him again.

'Oh, now, that all depends and don't little boys ask a lot of questions?'

They were walking very quickly, everyone was leaving the gardens and going off down the concrete slopes to tea, it was too cold for snow, she said, and he was out of breath now, with trying to keep up to her.

'But we might, and then again we might not, there might be treats in store, we might be seeing him somewhere else.'

'Where else? What sort of place?'

No answer.

'Doesn't he go to work?'

Nanny Fawcett rounded upon him alarmingly. 'Of course he goes to work, don't all honest men go to work, what do you take me for? I wouldn't have anything to do with any layabout, any idle man, you needn't imagine that I would.'

'No,' William said.

'But if we were to go and see him at work – well now, we might and that would be something!'

'What does he do?'

'Oh, something that would just surprise you.' Nanny Fawcett gripped his hand as they crossed the road at Kensington Gore. 'Something you'll never have heard of, and never would expect.'

'Tell me about it, *tell* me.'

'You'll find out soon enough, I daresay you will find out.'

Her face was flushed, set against the wind, and he dared not ask now, how her friend was different from all the rest, how he managed to escape her blanket condemnation of men. He had not looked any different. But perhaps he might learn the trick from him, if they met again, perhaps he could listen and watch, and discover the secret of Nanny Fawcett's favour.

He had tea in the oyster-grey drawing-room, with an

apricot Danish pastry brought in by his grandmother from Cadogan Square.

'We're not going to the Park today, we're going somewhere different. It's to be a treat.'

He was being dressed in best trousers and a white shirt, his mother had gone out. 'Mum's the word,' Nanny Fawcett had said. He wondered what to expect, dared not ask.

Outside a hotel, they stopped. Nanny Fawcett bent down to him. 'You're to enjoy yourself,' she said, pumping his hand up and down to emphasise her words. 'You're not to be a trouble. You go with my friend and do as you're told, and remember just how lucky you are.'

He looked up at her, prepared for anything at all. Nanny Fawcett laughed. 'Cow's eyes!' she said. 'You'll be the death of me. It's a *party*, isn't it?'

They walked up the wide, white marble steps of the hotel and through the revolving doors, and inside everything was hushed and softly lit from chandeliers, the carpets were rose-red on the floor. Nanny Fawcett held hard on to his hand. It was some minutes before her friend came, looking more than ever strange, in shirt sleeves, and with his hair combed flat back, as though he had been disturbed from a sleep, or in the middle of some job, up a ladder. William wondered if he lived in the hotel. He made a curious face at him, screwing the flesh up around his eyes and nose, and then letting it collapse again like a pile of ash, looking blandly at Nanny Fawcett.

'Well,' he said. 'It's all fixed up, you see, all arranged.'

'I wouldn't like to think that it was not,' said Nanny Fawcett.

He brayed with laughter, showing the long teeth.

'*We* were not coming to the back entrance,' Nanny Fawcett said.

The friend's hand shot out and pinched William's cheek, and he danced a little, on the balls of his feet.

'Time presses,' he said. 'We'll do well to be getting off, getting this one settled and so forth. Well, now ...' He winked.

'Get *along* ...' Nanny Fawcett gave him a little push in the back, 'and you mind your manners, I'll be around to collect you later, won't I?'

The friend waved his arm in the direction of a deserted lounge, full of green and gold armchairs. 'What about getting settled,' he said, 'having a nice tray of tea, what about you going and putting your feet up, and I'll be down directly.'

He took William's hand.

He had thought that the upstairs corridors of hotels led only to bedrooms, but when they emerged from the left, there were tall cream-painted pillars, and huge, fronded plants, and gilt mirrors, and they walked towards another lounge.

'Going to enjoy yourself?' the friend said.

William frowned.

'Well, don't have a lot to say, do you? Don't have much of a tongue in your head.'

He leered down horribly, the rubber face contorting itself and seeming to flush and darken; until a grin broke it open like a wave, and everything was different again. William wondered if the face changed in sleep, too.

'Where am I going?'

They stopped. The friend banged him lightly on the back. 'Well, to a *party*, aren't you? You're going to a party.'

'Oh. Is it your party?'

'It is not.'

A door swung open ahead, letting out voices.

'All you've to do, you've to mind what you say, then you'll be nice and dandy, you see, and nothing to do but enjoy yourself.'

He did not explain further.

At Christmas, there had been four parties, and none of them was at a hotel and all of them had terrified him, each time he had prayed that there would never be another. Now, he stood back behind Nanny Fawcett's friend, looking upon the room full of strangers, other children, in ribbon and net and velvet and white shirts under tartan ties, and his stomach clenched with dread. He did not know why he had been brought here.

'Well now, how very nice!' said the woman in mauve, bending down to him, 'How nice, dear! We were expecting you.' And she turned to the other, beside her. 'Our entertainer's child!' she said, and both of them laughed a little, and looked about the room for someone to take charge of him. 'His name is William,' she said.

He had thought that always one met the same people at parties, his cousin Sophie and the Cressett twins and fat Michael, but he knew nobody here at all, their names confused him and he hung back on the edge of their games.

'We've been told to be nice to you,' a boy said.

William stood, thinking of Nanny Fawcett and the friend, far away down all the carpeted stairs, eating tea in the empty lounge.

As it went on, it became like all the other parties he had known, the terrors were at least familiar, the awful taste of the tea and of trifles in little, waxed paper cases and the staring of the bigger girls. There were games which he did not win and dancing for which he had not brought his pumps. The woman in mauve clapped her hands and laughed a lot and changed the records on the gramophone, and from time to time, she took his hand and led him closer into the circle of the others. 'You are to look after this little boy, you are to be kind to William now, dear, try and remember.'

But then, suddenly, one of the hotel waiters had drawn the curtains and they were all made to sit tightly together on the carpeted floor, squealing a little with apprehension and excitement. Then the music began. Oh God, Oh God, make it not be a conjuror or a Punch and Judy, William thought, pressing his nails deeply into the palms of his hands. But it was not, it was something he had never seen before, something worse.

The area ahead of them was lit like a stage, with a high stool placed there, and then a figure came lumbering out of the darkness. From the shoulders down it was a man, his costume all in one piece and wumbling as it moved, like the covering on a panto-mime horse. But it stood upon only two legs and the legs were three times, ten times, as long as human legs, and oddly stiff at the joints. Above the shoulders, the huge head was not a man's head, but that of an elephant, nodding and bobbing and bending forward to the music and waving its disgusting trunk.

William sat and every so often closed his eyes, willing for it to be gone, for the curtains to be drawn again and the ordinary January daylight to flood the room. But he could still hear the music and when that stopped, the elephant man spoke and sang, the voice very deep, distorted and hollow, booming away inside the huge head. He opened his eyes and did not want to look, but he could not stop himself, the square of light and then the lurching animal man drew him. It was dancing, lifting its huge legs up and down stiffly, clapping its

hands together, while the head nodded. From somewhere, it produced a vividly coloured stuffed parrot,
which sat upon its shoulder and answered back to jokes,
in a terrible rasping voice. Then the music started
again.

'Now, children, now what about everybody doing a
little dance with me, what about us all dancing
together? Would you like that?'

'Yes,' they yelled. 'Yes, Yes!' and clapped and
bounced up and down.

'And what about somebody coming up on my
shoulder and being as high as the sky, what about that?
Would you like to do that?'

'Yes,' they screamed. 'Yes, yes!' and rushed forwards,
clamouring about the baggy legs, clutching and
laughing.

From the gramophone came the music for a Conga,
and the elephant man set off with everyone clinging on
behind in a chain, prancing about the room, and first
one, then another was lifted high up on to its great
shoulders, swaying with delight, hands touching the
ceiling, swinging the chandelier. William stood back
against the wall in the darkness, praying not to be
noticed, but when the line reached him, he was
noticed, the woman in mauve clucked and took his
hand, putting him in with the others, so that he was
forced to trot on one leg and then the next to the
music. And then, suddenly, he felt the elephant man
behind him, and he was lifted up, the hands digging
tightly into his sides, and he could neither scream nor
protest, he could scarcely breathe, only dangle
helplessly there, near to the cream-painted ceiling, and
see, far below him, the upturned mocking faces of the
others, hear the blast of the music. Through the slits in
the elephant head, he could see eyes, flickering like

lanterns in a turnip, and he looked away dizzy, praying to be set down.

At the end, the lights did not go on immediately, he could slip out of the door and nobody noticed him.

The corridor was silent, everything closed and secret. The music faded away as he ran, and found a flight of stairs and climbed them, not daring to look back. Here the passages were narrower, the carpets dark grey and thick as felt, so that his feet made no sound. There might have been nobody else in the building.

He had thought that he would die of fear, high up in the clutch of the elephant man, but he had not died, and now he must remember it, he could still hear the music and the shrieking of the others, pounding in his ears. He came up to a long mirror at the end of the corridor, and was terrified by his own reflection, tense and white-faced. The elephant man could be following him, might be anywhere at all, and perhaps there were others. He began to run, back down the stairs, but on the lower corridor heard voices and imagined some punishment inflicted upon him by the elephant man, or else by the hotel porters and maids, and the woman in mauve. He pushed open one of the grey doors in his panic. When the voices and footsteps had gone away, he would run again down to the lounge where Nanny Fawcett was having tea with her friend, it would be all right.

'Well, now!'

He spun round. It was a bedroom, with draped curtains and a light switched on over the long dressing-table, and reflected in the mirror, he saw the elephant man, arms up on either side of his head. He could not move, only stare in terror as the hands lifted off the grey head, up and up, and then down again, until it rested on his knees.

'Master William the party-boy,' said Nanny Fawcett's friend, and the face creased in sudden, wicked mirth, trembling and quivering. On a chair, William saw Nanny Fawcett's navy-blue coat and hat, and the sensible handbag. 'All a bit of a romp and a treat,' said her friend, 'blowed if it isn't!' His face crumpled into sadness and mock-weeping. 'Poor old elephant!'

William saw the two images separately, the face of the man, and that of the elephant on his lap, and then the reflections of them in the glass, he was surrounded by the terrible faces. He gave a sob, and put up a hand to shield his eyes, groping for the door-handle. It would not yield, something pushed him back, and then there was Nanny Fawcett, straightening her skirt, he was forced to go back into the room, while her friend the elephant man laughed until the tears ran down his cheeks. Outside in the corridor, the voices of the others, leaving the party.

'You didn't collect your present,' Nanny Fawcett said.

Because it was raining and the hotel was not near home, they went on a bus.

'You never would have guessed it, I know, never in a million years,' Nanny Fawcett said, her face flushed with pleasure. 'He used to be in the pantomimes and circuses, my friend, he's a very high-class entertainer.'

The lights of the cars swept down Piccadilly in a row, like an army advancing through the rain.

'You're the lucky one, aren't you, there's plenty that would envy you, I know. Going to a party and not even knowing the person! Well!'

He realised that he had not discovered for which child the party had been held.

'You've gone quiet,' she said, making him walk too

quickly round the Square. 'If you ate too much, I shan't be very pleased, shall I, after what I told you?'

He thought of the dreams he would have that night.

'Mum's the word,' Nanny Fawcett said, turning her key in the latch. For he must say nothing about her friend and nothing about the party.

He woke in the darkness to find his pillow, and the well of the bed below his neck, filled with vomit.

'The *next* time, you learn to hold back,' said Nanny Fawcett, stripping off his pyjamas. Her hair was twisted into curious plaits about her head. 'Your eyes are bigger than your stomach, so they are. The next time you just curb your greed, thank you very much.'

He stared into her face, and did not dare ask about 'the next time'. 'He's a very nice type of man,' she said, rubbing the cold sponge briskly about his face. 'Not at all the sort you would commonly meet, so mind your P's and Q's in future and play your cards right and you'll be going to quite a number of parties, I shouldn't wonder.'

Lying in the dark again, between stiff, clean sheets, he knew that since the day they drained the Round Pond, everything had surely changed and would never be as it was, and felt afraid, wishing for the time past, when Nanny Fawcett had despised all men.

The Case for the Defence

by Graham Greene

It was the strangest murder trial I ever attended. They named it the Peckham murder in the headlines, though Northwood Street, where the old woman was found battered to death, was not strictly speaking in Peckham. This was not one of those cases of circumstantial evidence in which you feel the jurymen's anxiety – because mistakes *have* been made – like domes of silence muting the court. No, this murderer was all but found with the body; no one present when the Crown counsel outlined his case believed that the man in the dock stood any chance at all.

He was a heavy stout man with bulging bloodshot eyes. All his muscles seemed to be in his thighs. Yes, an ugly customer, one you wouldn't forget in a hurry – and that was an important point because the Crown proposed to call four witnesses who hadn't forgotten him, who had seen him hurrying away from the little red villa in Northwood Street. The clock had just struck two in the morning.

Mrs Salmon in 15 Northwood Street had been unable to sleep; she heard a door click shut and thought it was her own gate. So she went to the window and saw Adams (that was his name) on the steps of Mrs Parker's house. He had just come out and he was wearing gloves. He had a hammer in his hand and she saw him drop it into the laurel bushes by the front gate. But before he moved away, he had looked up – at her window. The fatal instinct that tells a man when he is watched exposed him in the light of a street-lamp to her gaze – his eyes suffused with horrifying and brutal fear, like an animal's when you raise a whip. I talked afterwards to Mrs Salmon, who naturally after the astonishing verdict went in fear herself. As I imagine did all the witnesses – Henry MacDougall, who had been driving home from Benfleet late and nearly ran Adams down at the corner of Northwood Street. Adams was walking in the middle of the road looking dazed. And old Mr Wheeler, who lived next door to Mrs Parker, at No. 12, and was wakened by a noise – like a chair falling – through the thin-as-paper villa wall, and got up and looked out of the window, just as Mrs Salmon had done, saw Adams's back and, as he turned, those bulging eyes. In Laurel Avenue he had been seen by yet another witness – his luck was badly out; he might as well have committed the crime in broad daylight.

'I understand,' counsel said, 'that the defence proposes to plead mistaken identity. Adams's wife will tell you that he was with her at two in the morning on February 14, but after you have heard the witnesses for the Crown and examined carefully the features of the prisoner, I do not think you will be prepared to admit the possibility of a mistake.'

It was all over, you would have said, but the hanging.

After the formal evidence had been given by the policeman who had found the body and the surgeon who examined it, Mrs Salmon was called. She was the ideal witness, with her slight Scotch accent and her expression of honesty, care and kindness.

The counsel for the Crown brought the story gently out. She spoke very firmly. There was no malice in her, and no sense of importance at standing there in the Central Criminal Court with a judge in scarlet hanging on her words and the reporters writing them down. Yes, she said, and then she had gone downstairs and rung up the police station.

'And do you see the man here in court?'

She looked straight at the big man in the dock, who stared hard at her with his pekingese eyes without emotion.

'Yes,' she said, 'there he is.'

'You are quite certain?'

She said simply, 'I couldn't be mistaken, sir.'

It was all as easy as that.

'Thank you, Mrs Salmon.'

Counsel for the defence rose to cross-examine. If you had reported as many murder trials as I have, you would have known beforehand what line he would take. And I was right, up to a point.

'Now, Mrs Salmon, you must remember that a man's life may depend on your evidence.'

'I do remember it, sir.'

'Is your eyesight good?'

'I have never had to wear spectacles, sir.'

'You are a woman of fifty-five?'

'Fifty-six, sir.'

'And the man you saw was on the other side of the road?'

'Yes, sir.'

'And it was two o'clock in the morning. You must have remarkable eyes, Mrs Salmon?'

'No, sir. There was moonlight, and when the man looked up, he had the lamplight on his face.'

'And you have no doubt whatever that the man you saw is the prisoner?'

I couldn't make out what he was at. He couldn't have expected any other answer than the one he got.

'None whatever, sir. It isn't a face one forgets.'

Counsel took a look round the court for a moment. Then he said, 'Do you mind, Mrs Salmon, examining again the people in court? No, not the prisoner. Stand up, please, Mr Adams,' and there at the back of the court with thick stout body and muscular legs and a pair of bulging eyes, was the exact image of the man in the dock. He was even dressed the same – tight blue suit and striped tie.

'Now think very carefully, Mrs Salmon. Can you still swear that the man you saw drop the hammer in Mrs Parker's garden was the prisoner – and not this man, who is his twin brother?'

Of course she couldn't. She looked from one to the other and didn't say a word.

There the big brute sat in the dock with his legs crossed, and there he stood too at the back of the court and they both stared at Mrs Salmon. She shook her head.

What we saw then was the end of the case. There wasn't a witness prepared to swear that it was the prisoner he'd seen. And the brother? He had his alibi, too; he was with his wife.

And so the man was acquitted for lack of evidence. But whether – if he did the murder and not his brother – he was punished or not, I don't know. That extraordinary day had an extraordinary end. I followed Mrs Salmon out of court and we got wedged in the crowd who were waiting, of course, for the twins. The police tried to drive the crowd away, but all they could do was keep the road-way clear for traffic. I learned later that they tried to get the twins to leave by a back way, but they wouldn't. One of them – no one knew which – said, 'I've been acquitted, haven't I?' and they walked bang out of the front entrance. Then it happened. I don't know how, though I was only six feet away. The crowd moved and somehow one of the twins got pushed on to the road right in front of a bus.

He gave a squeal like a rabbit and that was all; he was dead, his skull smashed just as Mrs Parker's had been. Divine vengeance? I wish I knew. There was the other Adams getting on his feet from beside the body and looking straight over at Mrs Salmon. He was crying, but whether he was the murderer or the innocent man nobody will ever be able to tell. But if you were Mrs Salmon, could you sleep at night?

The Tell-Tale Heart

by Edgar Allan Poe

True! – nervous – very, very dreadfully nervous I had been and am; but why *will* you say that I am mad? The disease had sharpened my senses – not destroyed – not dulled them. Above all was the sense of hearing acute. I heard all things in the heaven and in the earth. I heard many things in hell. How, then, am I mad? Hearken! and observe how healthily – how calmly I can tell you the whole story.

It is impossible to say how first the idea entered my brain; but once conceived, it haunted me day and night. Object there was none. Passion there was none. I loved the old man. He had never wronged me. He had never given me insult. For his gold I had no desire. I think it was his eye! yes, it was this! One of his eyes resembled that of a vulture – a pale blue eye, with a film over it. Whenever it fell upon me, my blood ran cold; and so by degrees – very gradually – I made up my mind to take the life of the old man, and thus rid myself of the eye for ever.

Now this is the point. You fancy me mad. Madmen know nothing. But you should have seen *me*. You should have seen how wisely I proceeded – with what caution – with what foresight – with what dissimulation[1] I went to work! I was never kinder to the old man than during the whole week before I killed him. And every night,

[1] secrecy

about midnight, I turned the latch of his door and opened it – oh, so gently! And then, when I had made an opening sufficient for my head, I put in a dark lantern, all closed, closed so that no light shone out, and then I thrust in my head. Oh, you would have laughed to see how cunningly I thrust it in! I moved it slowly – very, very slowly, so that I might not disturb the old man's sleep. It took me an hour to place my whole head within the opening so far that I could see him as he lay upon his bed. Ha! – would a madman have been so wise as this? And then, when my head was well in the room, I undid the lantern cautiously – oh, so cautiously – cautiously (for the hinges creaked) – I undid it just so much that a single thin ray fell upon the vulture eye. And this I did for seven long nights – every night just at midnight – but I found the eye always closed; and so it was impossible to do the work; for it was not the old man who vexed me, but his Evil Eye. And every morning, when the day broke, I went boldly into the chamber, and spoke courageously to him, calling him by name in a hearty tone, and enquiring how he had passed the night. So you see he would have been a very profound old man, indeed, to suspect that every night, just at twelve, I looked in upon him while he slept.

Upon the eighth night I was more than usually cautious in opening the door. A watch's minute hand moves more quickly than did mine. Never before that night had I *felt* the extent of my own powers – of my sagacity.[2] I could scarcely contain my feelings of triumph. To think that there I was, opening the door, little by little, and he not even to dream of my secret deeds or thoughts. I fairly chuckled at the idea; and perhaps he heard me; for he moved on the bed

[2] wisdom

suddenly, as if startled. Now you may think that I drew back – but no. His room was as black as pitch with the thick darkness (for the shutters were close fastened, through fear of robbers), and so I knew that he could not see the opening of the door, and I kept pushing it on steadily, steadily.

I had my head in, and was about to open the lantern, when my thumb slipped upon the tin fastening, and the old man sprang up in the bed, crying out – 'Who's there?'

I kept quite still and said nothing. For a whole hour I did not move a muscle, and in the mean time I did not hear him lie down. He was still sitting up in the bed listening; just as I have done, night after night, hearkening to the death watches in the wall.

Presently I heard a slight groan, and I knew it was the groan of mortal terror. It was not a groan of pain or of grief – oh, no! – it was the low stifled sound that arises from the bottom of the soul when overcharged with awe. I knew the sound well. Many a night, just at midnight, when all the world slept, it has welled up from my own bosom, deepening, with its dreadful echo, the terrors that distracted me. I say I knew it well. I knew what the old man felt, and pitied him, although I chuckled at heart. I knew that he had been lying awake ever since the first slight noise, when he had turned in the bed. His fears had been ever since growing upon him. He had been trying to fancy them causeless, but could not. He had been saying to himself – 'It is nothing but the wind in the chimney – it is only a mouse crossing the floor,' or 'it is merely a cricket which has made a single chirp.' Yes, he had been trying to comfort himself with these suppositions; but he had found all in vain. *All in vain*; because Death, in approaching him, had stalked with his black shadow before him, and enveloped the victim. And it was the mournful influence of the unperceived shadow that caused him to feel – although he neither saw nor heard – to *feel* the presence of my head within the room.

When I had waited a long time, very patiently, without hearing him lie down, I resolved to open a little – a very, very little crevice in the lantern. So I opened it – you cannot imagine how stealthily,[3] stealthily – until, at length, a single dim ray, like the thread of the spider, shot from out the crevice and full upon the vulture eye.

It was open – wide, wide open – and I grew furious as I gazed upon it. I saw it with perfect distinctness – all a dull blue, with a hideous veil over it that chilled the very marrow in my bones; but I could see nothing else of the old man's face or person: for I had directed the ray as if by instinct, precisely upon the damned spot.

And now have I not told you that what you mistake for madness is but over-acuteness of the senses? – now, I say, there came to my ears a low, dull, quick sound, such as a watch makes when enveloped in cotton. I knew *that* sound well too. It was the beating of the old man's heart. It increased my fury, as the beating of a drum stimulates the soldier into courage.

But even yet I refrained and kept still. I scarcely breathed. I held the lantern motionless. I tried how steadily I could maintain the ray upon the eye. Meantime the hellish tattoo[4] of the heart increased. It grew quicker and quicker, and louder and louder every instant. The old man's terror *must* have been extreme! It grew louder, I say, louder every moment! – do you mark me well? I have told you that I am nervous: so I am. And now at the dead hour of the night, amid the dreadful

---

[3] cautiously
[4] rhythm (as in the beating of a drum)

silence of that old house, so strange a noise as this excited me to uncontrollable terror. Yet, for some minutes longer I refrained and stood still. But the beating grew louder, louder! I thought the heart must burst. And now a new anxiety seized me – the sound would be heard by a neighbour! The old man's hour had come! With a loud yell, I threw open the lantern and leaped into the room. He shrieked once – once only. In an instant I dragged him to the floor, and pulled the heavy bed over him. I then smiled gaily, to find the deed so far done. But, for many minutes, the heart beat on with a muffled sound. This, however, did not vex me, it would not be heard through the wall. At length it ceased. The old man was dead. I removed the bed and examined the corpse. Yes, he was stone, stone dead. I placed my hand upon the heart and held it there many minutes. There was no pulsation. He was stone dead. His eye would trouble me no more.

If still you think me mad, you will think so no longer when I describe the wise precautions I took for the concealment of the body. The night waned, and I worked hastily, but in silence. First of all I dismembered the corpse. I cut off the head and the arms and the legs.

I then took up three planks from the flooring of the chamber, and deposited all between the scantlings. I then replaced the boards so cleverly, so cunningly, that no human eye – not even *his* – could have detected anything wrong. There was nothing to wash out – no stain of any kind – no blood-spot whatever. I had been too wary for that. A tub had caught all – ha! ha!

When I had made an end of these labours, it was four o'clock – still dark as midnight. As the bell sounded the hour, there came a knocking at the street door. I went down to open it with a light heart – for what had I *now* to fear? There entered three men, who introduced themselves, with perfect suavity, as officers of the police. A shriek had been heard by a neighbour during the night; suspicion of foul play had been aroused; information had been lodged at the police office, and they (the officers) had been deputed to search the premises.

I smiled – for *what* had I to fear? I bade the gentlemen welcome. The shriek, I said, was my own in a dream. The old man, I mentioned, was absent in the country. I took my visitors all over the house. I bade them search – search *well*. I led them, at length, to *his* chamber. I showed them *his* treasures secure, undisturbed. In the enthusiasm of my confidence, I brought chairs into the room, and desired them *here* to rest from their fatigues, while I myself, in the wild audacity of my perfect triumph, placed my own seat upon the very spot beneath which reposed the corpse of the victim.

The officers were satisfied. My *manner* had convinced them. I was singularly at ease. They sat, and while I answered cheerily, they chatted of familiar things. But, ere long, I felt myself getting pale and wished them gone. My head ached, and I fancied a ringing in my ears: but still they sat and still they chatted. The ringing became more distinct: it continued and became more distinct: I talked more freely to get rid of the feeling: but it continued and gained definitiveness – until, at length, I found that the noise was *not* within my ears.

No doubt I now grew *very* pale; but I talked more fluently, and with a heightened voice. Yet the sound increased – and what could I do? It was *a low, dull, quick sound – much such a sound as a watch makes when enveloped in cotton*. I gasped for breath – and yet the officers heard it not. I talked more quickly – and vehemently; but the noise steadily increased. I arose and argued about trifles, in a high key and with violent gesticulations, but the noise steadily increased. Why *would* they not be gone? I paced the floor to and fro with heavy strides, as if excited to fury by the observation of the men – but the noise steadily increased. Oh God! what *could* I do? I foamed – I raved – I swore! I swung the chair upon which I had been sitting, and grated it upon the boards, but the noise arose over all and continually increased. It grew louder – louder – *louder*! And still the men chatted pleasantly, and smiled. Was it possible they heard not? Almighty God! – no, no! They heard! – they suspected! – they *knew*! – they were making a mockery of my horror! – this I thought, and this I think. But anything was better than this agony! Anything was more tolerable than this derision! I could bear those hypocritical smiles no longer! I felt that I must scream or die! – and now – again! – hark! louder! louder! louder! *louder*! –

'Villains!' I shrieked, 'dissemble[5] no more! I admit the deed! – tear up the planks! – here, here! – it is the beating of his hideous heart!'

[5] pretend

The Wounded Cormorant

by Liam O'Flaherty

Beneath the great grey cliff of Clogher Mor there was a massive square black rock, dotted with white limpets, sitting in the sea. The sea rose and fell about it frothing. Rising, the sea hoisted the seaweed that grew along the rock's rims until the long red winding strands spread like streams of blood through the white foam. Falling, the tide sucked the strands down taut from their bulbous roots.

Silence. It was noon. The sea was calm. Rock-birds slept on its surface, their beaks resting on their fat white breasts. Tall sea-gulls standing on one leg dozed high up in the ledges of the cliff. On the great rock there was a flock of black cormorants resting, bobbing their long necks to draw the food from their swollen gullets.

Above on the cliff-top a yellow goat was looking down into the sea. She suddenly took fright. She snorted and turned towards the crag at a smart run. Turning, her hoof loosed a flat stone from the cliff's edge. The stone fell, whirling, on to the rock where the cormorants rested. It fell among them with a crash and arose in fragments. The birds swooped into the air. As they rose a fragment of the stone struck one of them in the right leg. The leg was broken. The wounded bird uttered a shrill scream and dropped the leg. As the bird flew outwards from the rock the leg dangled crookedly.

The flock of cormorants did not fly far. As soon as they passed the edge of the rock they dived headlong into the sea. Their long black bodies, with outstretched necks, passed rapidly beneath the surface of the waves, a long way, before they rose again, shaking the brine from their heads. Then they sat in the sea, their black backs shimmering in the sunlight, their pale brown throats thrust forward, their tiny heads poised on their curved long necks. They sat watching, like upright snakes, trying to discover whether there were any enemies near. Seeing nothing, they began to cackle and flutter their feathers.

But the wounded one rushed about in the water flapping its wings in agony. The salt brine stung the wound, and it could not stand still. After a few moments it rose from the sea and set off at a terrific rate, flying along the face of the cliff, mad with pain. It circled the face of the cliff three times, flying in enormous arcs, as if it were trying to flee from the pain in its leg. Then it swooped down again towards the flock and alighted in the water beside them.

The other birds noticed it and began to cackle. It swam close to one bird, but that bird shrieked and darted away from it. It approached another bird, and that bird prodded it viciously with its beak. Then all the birds screamed simultaneously and rose from the water, with a great swish of their long wings. The wounded one rose with them. They flew up to the rock again and alighted on it, bobbing their necks anxiously and peering in all directions, still slightly terrified by the stone that had fallen there. The wounded one alighted on the rocks with them, tried to stand up, and immediately fell on its stomach. But it struggled up again and stood on its unwounded leg.

The other birds, having assured themselves that there was no enemy near, began to look at the wounded one suspiciously. It had its eyes closed, and it was wobbling unstably on its leg. They saw the wounded leg hanging crookedly from its belly and its wings trailing slightly. They began to make curious screaming noises. One bird trotted over to the wounded one and pecked at it. The wounded bird uttered a low scream and fell forward on its chest. It spread out its wings, turned up its beak, and opened it out wide, like a young bird in a nest demanding food.

Immediately the whole flock raised a cackle again and took to their wings. They flew out to sea, high up in the air. The wounded bird struggled up and also took flight after them. But they were far ahead of it, and it could not catch up with them on account of its waning strength. However, they soon wheeled inwards towards the cliff, and it wheeled in after them, all flying low over the water's surface. Then the flock rose slowly, fighting the air fiercely with their long thin wings in order to propel their heavy bodies upwards. They flew half-way up the face of the cliff and alighted on a wide ledge that was dotted with little black pools and white feathers strewn about.

The wounded bird tried to rise too, but it had not gone out to sea far enough in its swoop. Therefore it had not gathered sufficient speed to carry it up to their ledge. It breasted the cliff ten yards below the ledge, and being unable to rise upwards by banking, it had to wheel outwards again, cackling wildly. It flew out very far, descending to the surface of the sea until the tips of its wings touched the water. Then it wheeled inwards once more, rising gradually, making a tremendous effort to gather enough speed to take it to the ledge where its comrades rested. At all costs it must reach them or perish. Cast out from the flock, death was certain. Sea-gulls would devour it.

When the other birds saw it coming towards them

and heard the sharp whirring of its wings as it rose strongly, they began to cackle fiercely, and came in a close line to the brink of the ledge, darting their beaks forward and shivering. The approaching bird cackled also and came headlong at them. It flopped on to the ledge over their backs and screamed, lying on the rock helplessly with its wings spread out quite exhausted. But they had no mercy. They fell upon it fiercely, tearing at its body with their beaks, plucking out its black feathers and rooting it about with their feet. It struggled madly to creep in farther on the ledge, trying to get into a dark crevice in the cliff to hide, but they dragged it back again and pushed it towards the brink of the ledge. One bird prodded its right eye with its beak. Another gripped the broken leg firmly in its beak and tore at it.

At last the wounded bird lay on its side and began to tremble, offering no resistance to their attacks. Then they cackled loudly, and, dragging it to the brink of the ledge they hurled it down. It fell fluttering feebly through the air, slowly descending, turning round and round, closing and opening its wings, until it reached the sea.

Then it fluttered its wings twice and lay still. An advancing wave dashed it against the side of the black rock and then it disappeared, sucked down among the seaweed strands.

The Dress

by Dylan Thomas

They had followed him for two days over the length of
the country, but he had lost them at the foot of the
hills, and, hidden in a golden bush, had heard them
shouting as they stumbled down the valley. Behind a
tree on the ridge of the hills he had peeped down on to
the fields where they hurried about like dogs, where
they poked the hedges with their sticks and set up a
faint howling as a mist came suddenly from the spring
sky and hid them from his eyes. But the mist was a
mother to him, putting a coat around his shoulders
where the shirt was torn and the blood dry on his
blades. The mist made him warm; he had the food and
the drink of the mist on his lips; and he smiled through
her mantle[1] like a cat. He worked away from the valley-
wards side of the hill into the denser trees that might
lead him to light and fire and a basin of soup. He
thought of the coals that might be hissing in the grate,
and of the young mother standing alone. He thought of
her hair. Such a nest it would make for his hands. He
ran through the trees and found himself on a narrow
road. Which way should he walk; towards or away from
the moon? The mist had made a secret of the position
of the moon, but, in a corner of the sky, where the mist
had fallen apart, he could see the angles of the stars. He
walked   towards   the   north   where   the   stars   were,

[1] cloak

mumbling a song with no tune, hearing his feet suck in and out of the spongy earth.

Now there was time to collect his thoughts, but no sooner had he started to set them in order than an owl made a cry in the trees that hung over the road, and he stopped and winked up at her, finding a mutual melancholy[2] in her sounds. Soon she would swoop and fasten on a mouse. He saw her for a moment as she sat screeching on her bough. Then, frightened of her, he hurried on, and had not gone more than a few yards into the darkness when, with a fresh cry, she flew away. Pity the hare, he thought, for the weasel will drink her. The road sloped to the stars, and the trees and the valleys and the memory of the guns faded behind.

He heard footsteps. An old man, radiant with rain, stepped out of the mist.

Good night, sir, said the old man.

No night for the son of woman, said the madman.

The old man whistled, and hurried, half running, in the direction of the roadside trees.

Let the hounds know, the madman chuckled as he climbed up the hill, Let the hounds know. And, crafty as a fox, he doubled back to where the misty road branched off three ways. Hell on the stars, he said, and walked towards the dark.

The world was a ball under his feet; it kicked as he ran; it dropped; up came the trees. In the distance a poacher's dog yelled at the trap on its foot, and he heard it and ran the faster, thinking the enemy was on his heels. Duck, boys, duck, he called out, but with the voice of one who might have pointed to a fallen star.

Remembering of a sudden that he had not slept since

[2] sadness

the escape, he left off running. Now the waters of the rain, too tired to strike the earth, broke up as they fell and blew about in the wind like the sandman's grains. If he met sleep, sleep would be a girl. For the last two nights, while walking or running over the empty county, he had dreamed of their meeting. Lie down, she would say, and would give him her dress to lie on, stretching herself out by his side. Even as he had dreamed, and the twigs under his running feet had made a noise like the rustle of her dress, the enemy had shouted in the fields. He had run on and on, leaving sleep farther behind him. Sometimes there was a sun, a moon, and sometimes under a black sky he had tossed and thrown the wind before he could be off.

Where is Jack? they asked in the gardens of the place he had left. Up on the hills with a butcher's knife, they said, smiling. But the knife was gone, thrown at a tree and quivering there still. There was no heat in his head. He ran on and on, howling for sleep.

And she, alone in the house, was sewing her new dress. It was a bright country dress with flowers on the bodice. Only a few more stitches were needed before it would be ready to wear. It would lie neat on her shoulders, and two of the flowers would be growing out of her breasts.

When she walked with her husband on Sunday mornings over the fields and down into the village, the boys would smile at her behind their hands, and the shaping of the dress round her belly would set all the widow women talking. She slipped into her new dress, and, looking into the mirror over the fireplace, saw that it was prettier than she had imagined. It made her face paler and her long hair darker. She had cut it low.

A dog out in the night lifted its head up and howled.

She turned away hurriedly from her reflection, and pulled the curtains closer.

Out in the night they were searching for a madman. He had green eyes, they said, and had married a lady. They said he had cut off her lips because she smiled at men. They took him away, but he stole a knife from the kitchen and slashed his keeper and broke out into the wild valleys.

From afar he saw the light in the house, and stumbled up to the edge of the garden. He felt, he did not see, the little fence around it. The rusting wire scraped on his hands and the wet, abominable grass crept over his knees. And once he was through the fence, the hosts of the garden came rushing to meet him, the flower-headed, and the bodying frosts. He had torn his fingers while the old wounds were still wet. Like a man of blood he came out of the enemy's darkness on to the steps. He said in a whisper, Let them not shoot me. And he opened the door.

She was in the middle of the room. Her hair had fallen untidily, and three of the buttons at the neck of her dress were undone. What made the dog howl as it did? Frightened of the howling, and thinking of the tales she had heard, she rocked in her chair. What became of the woman? she wondered as she rocked. She could not think of a woman without any lips. What became of women without any lips? she wondered.

The door made no noise. He stepped into the room, trying to smile, and, holding out his hands.

Oh, you've come back, she said.

Then she turned in her chair and saw him. There was blood even by his green eyes. She put her fingers to her mouth. Not shoot, he said.

But the moving of her arm drew the neck of her dress apart, and he stared in wonder at her wide, white forehead, her frightened eyes and mouth, and down on to the flowers on her dress. With the moving of her arm, her dress danced in the light. She sat before him, covered in flowers. Sleep, said the madman. And, kneeling down, he put his bewildered head upon her lap.

The Half-Brothers

by Elizabeth Gaskell

My mother was twice married. She never spoke of her first husband, and it is only from other people that I have learnt what little I know about him. I believe she was scarcely seventeen when she was married to him: and he was barely one-and-twenty. He rented a small farm up in Cumberland, somewhere towards the sea-coast; but he was perhaps too young and inexperienced to have the charge of land and cattle; anyhow, his affairs did not prosper, and he fell into ill-health, and died of consumption[1] before they had been three years man and wife, leaving my mother a young widow of twenty, with a little child only just able to walk, and the farm on her hands for four years more by the lease, with half the stock on it dead, or sold off one by one to pay the more pressing debts, and with no money to purchase more, or even to buy the provisions needed for the small consumption of every day. There was another child coming, too; and sad and sorry, I believe, she was to think of it.

A dreary winter she must have had in her lonesome dwelling, with never another near it for miles around; her sister came to bear her company, and they two planned and plotted how to make every penny they could raise go as far as possible. I can't tell you how it happened that my little sister, whom I never saw, came

[1] a disease of the lungs, also called tuberculosis

85

to sicken and die; but, as if my poor mother's cup was not full enough, only a fortnight before Gregory was born the little girl took ill of scarlet fever, and in a week she lay dead.

My mother was, I believe, just stunned with this last blow. My aunt has told me that she did not cry; Aunt Fanny would have been thankful if she had; but she sat holding the poor wee lassie's hand, and looking in her pretty, pale, dead face, without so much as shedding a tear. And it was all the same, when they had to take her away to be buried. She just kissed the child, and sat her down in the window-seat to watch the little black train of people (neighbours – my aunt, and one far-off cousin, who were all the friends they could muster) go winding away amongst the snow, which had fallen thinly over the country the night before.

When my aunt came back from the funeral, she found my mother in the same place, and as dry-eyed as ever. So she continued until after Gregory was born; and, somehow, his coming seemed to loosen the tears, and she cried day and night, day and night, till my aunt and the other watcher looked at each other in dismay, and would fain[2] have stopped her if they had but known how. But she bade them let her alone, and not be over-anxious, for every drop she shed eased her brain, which had been in a terrible state before for want of the power to cry. She seemed after that to think of nothing but her new little baby; she hardly appeared to remember either her husband or her little daughter that lay dead in Brigham churchyard – at least so Aunt Fanny said; but she was a great talker, and my mother was very silent by nature, and I think Aunt Fanny may have been mistaken in believing that my mother never

[2] gladly

thought of her husband and child just because she never spoke about them.

Aunt Fanny was older than my mother, and had a way of treating her like a child; but, for all that, she was a kind, warm-hearted creature, who thought more of her sister's welfare than she did of her own; and it was on her bit of money that they principally lived, and on what the two could earn by working for the great Glasgow sewing-merchants. But by-and-by my mother's eyesight began to fail. It was not that she was exactly blind, for she could see well enough to guide herself about the house, and to do a good deal of domestic work; but she could no longer do fine sewing and earn money. It must have been with the heavy crying she had had in her day, for she was but a young creature at this time, and as pretty a young woman, I have heard people say, as any on the countryside.

She took it sadly to heart that she could no longer gain anything towards the keep of herself and her child. My Aunt Fanny would fain have persuaded her that she had enough to do in managing their cottage and minding Gregory; but my mother knew that they were pinched, and that Aunt Fanny herself had not as much to eat, even of the commonest kind of food, as she could have done with; and as for Gregory, he was not a strong lad, and needed, not more food – for he always had enough, whoever went short – but better nourishment, and more flesh-meat.

One day – it was Aunt Fanny who told me all this about my poor mother, long after her death – as the sisters were sitting together, Aunt Fanny working, and my mother hushing Gregory to sleep, William Preston, who was afterwards my father, came in.

He was reckoned an old bachelor; I suppose he was long past forty, and he was one of the wealthiest farmers thereabouts, and had known my grandfather well, and my mother and my aunt in their more prosperous days. He sat down, and began to twirl his hat by way of being agreeable; my Aunt Fanny talked, and he listened and looked at my mother. But he said very little, either on that visit, or on many another that he paid before he spoke out what had been the real purpose of his calling so often all along, and from the very first time he came to their house.

One Sunday, however, my Aunt Fanny stayed away from church, and took care of the child, and my mother went alone. When she came back, she ran straight upstairs, without going into the kitchen to look at Gregory or speak any word to her sister, and Aunt Fanny heard her cry as if her heart was breaking; so she went up and scolded her right well through the bolted door, till at last she got her to open it. And then she threw herself on my aunt's neck, and told her that William Preston had asked her to marry him, and had promised to take good charge of her boy, and to let him want for nothing, neither in the way of keep nor of education, and that she had consented.

Aunt Fanny was a good deal shocked at this; for, as I have said, she had often thought that my mother had forgotten her first husband very quickly, and now here was proof positive of it, if she could so soon think of marrying again. Besides, as Aunt Fanny used to say, she herself would have been a far more suitable match for a man of William Preston's age than Helen, who, though she was a widow, had not seen her four-and twentieth summer.

However, as Aunt Fanny said, they had not asked her advice; and there was much to be said on the other side of the question. Helen's eyesight would never be good for much again, and as William Preston's wife she would never need to do anything, if she chose to sit with her hands before her; and a boy was a great charge to a widowed mother; and now there would be a decent, steady man to see after him. So, by-and-by, Aunt Fanny seemed to take a brighter view of the marriage than did my mother herself, who hardly ever looked up, and never smiled after the day when she promised William Preston to be his wife. But much as she had loved Gregory before, she seemed to love him more now. She was continually talking to him when they were alone, though he was far too young to understand her moaning words, or give her any comfort, except by his caresses.

At last William Preston and she were wed; and she went to be mistress of a well-stocked house, not above half an hour's walk from where Aunt Fanny lived. I believe she did all that she could to please my father; and a more dutiful wife, I have heard him himself say, could never have been. But she did not love him, and he soon found it out. She loved Gregory, and she did not love him.

Perhaps, love would have come in time, if he had been patient enough to wait; but it just turned him sour to see how her eye brightened and her colour came at the sight of that little child, while for him who had given her so much, she had only gentle words as cold as ice. He got to taunt her with the difference in her manner, as if that would bring love: and he took a positive dislike to Gregory – he was so jealous of the ready love that always gushed out like a spring of fresh water when he came near. He wanted her to love him more, and perhaps that was all well and good; but he wanted her to love her child less, and that was an evil wish.

One day, he gave way to his temper, and cursed and

swore at Gregory, who had got into some mischief, as children will; my mother made some excuse for him; my father said it was hard enough to have to keep another man's child, without having it perpetually held up in its naughtiness by his wife, who ought to be always in the same mind that he was; and so from little they got to more; and the end of it was, that my mother took to her bed before her time, and I was born that very day.

My father was glad, and proud, and sorry, all in a breath; glad and proud that a son was born to him; and sorry for his poor wife's state, and to think how his angry words had brought it on. But he was a man who liked better to be angry than sorry, so he soon found out that it was all Gregory's fault, and owed him an additional grudge for having hastened my birth.

He had another grudge against him before long. My mother began to sink the day after I was born. My father sent to Carlisle for doctors, and would have coined his heart's blood into gold to save her, if that could have been; but it could not.

My Aunt Fanny used to say sometimes, that she thought that Helen did not wish to live, and so just let herself die away without trying to take hold on life; but when I questioned her, she owned that my mother did all the doctors bade her do, with the same sort of uncomplaining patience with which she had acted through life. One of her last requests was to have Gregory laid in her bed by my side, and then she made him take hold of my little hand. Her husband came in while she was looking at us so, and when he bent tenderly over her to ask her how she felt now, and seemed to gaze on us two little half-brothers, with a grave sort of kindliness, she looked up in his face and smiled, almost her first smile at him; and such a sweet smile! as more besides Aunt Fanny have said.

In an hour she was dead. Aunt Fanny came to live with us. It was the best thing that could be done. My father would have been glad to return to his old mode of bachelor life, but what could he do with two little children? He heeded a woman to take care of him, and who so fitting as his wife's elder sister? So she had the charge of me from my birth; and for a time I was weakly, as was but natural, and she was always beside me, night and day watching over me, and my father nearly as anxious as she. For his land had come down from father to son for more than three hundred years, and he would have cared for me merely as his flesh and blood that was to inherit the land after him.

But he needed something to love, for all that, to most people, he was a stern, hard man, and he took to me as, I fancy, he had taken to no human being before – as he might have taken to my mother, if she had had no former life for him to be jealous of. I loved him back again right heartily. I loved all around me, I believe, for everybody was kind to me. After a time, I overcame my original weakliness of constitution, and was just a bonny, strong-looking lad whom every passer-by noticed, when my father took me with him to the nearest town.

At home I was the darling of my aunt, the tenderly-beloved of my father, the pet and plaything of the old domestic, the 'young master' of the farm-labourers, before whom I played many a lordly antic, assuming a sort of authority which sat oddly enough, I doubt not, on such a baby as I was.

Gregory was three years older than I. Aunt Fanny was always kind to him in deed and in action, but she did not often think about him, she had fallen so completely into the habit of being engrossed by me, from the fact of my having come into her charge as a delicate baby. My father never got over his grudging dislike to his stepson, who had so innocently wrestled with him for the possession of my mother's heart. I mistrust me, too, that my father always considered him as the cause of my mother's death and my early delicacy; and utterly unreasonable as this may seem, I believe my father rather cherished his feeling of alienation to my brother as a duty, than strove to repress it.

Yet not for the world would my father have grudged him anything that money could purchase. That was, as it were, in the bond when he had wedded my mother. Gregory was lumpish and loutish, awkward and ungainly, marring[3] whatever he meddled in, and many a hard word and sharp scolding did he get from the people about the farm, who hardly waited till my father's back was turned before they rated the stepson.

I am ashamed – my heart is sore to think how I fell into the fashion of the family, and slighted my poor orphan stepbrother. I don't think I ever scouted him,[4] or was wilfully ill-natured to him; but the habit of being considered in all things, and being treated as something uncommon and superior, made me insolent in my prosperity, and I exacted more than Gregory was always willing to grant, and then, irritated, I sometimes repeated the disparaging[5] words I had heard others use with regard to him, without fully understanding their meaning. Whether he did or not I cannot tell. I am afraid he did. He used to turn silent and quiet – sullen and sulky, my father thought it; stupid, Aunt Fanny used to call it.

But everyone said he was stupid and dull, and this stupidity and dulness grew upon him. He would sit without speaking a word, sometimes, for hours; then

[3] spoiling
[4] mocked him
[5] critical

my father would bid him rise and do some piece of work, maybe, about the farm. And he would take three or four tellings before he would go. When we were sent to school, it was all the same. He could never be made to remember his lessons; the schoolmaster grew weary of scolding and flogging, and at last advised my father just to take him away, and set him to some farmwork that might not be above his comprehension. I think he was more gloomy and stupid than ever after this, yet he was not a cross lad; he was patient and good-natured, and would try to do a kind turn for any one, even if they had been scolding or cuffing him not a minute before. But very often his attempts at kindness ended in some mischief to the very people he was trying to serve, owing to his awkward, ungainly ways.

I suppose I was a clever lad; at any rate, I always got plenty of praise; and was, as we called it, the cock of the school. The schoolmaster said I could learn anything I chose, but my father, who had no great learning himself, saw little use in much for me, and took me away betimes, and kept me with him about the farm. Gregory was made into a kind of shepherd, receiving his training under old Adam, who was nearly past his work. I think old Adam was almost the first person who had a good opinion of Gregory. He stood to it that my brother had good parts, though he did not rightly know how to bring them out; and, for knowing the bearings of the Fells, he said he had never seen a lad like him. My father would try to bring Adam round to speak of Gregory's faults and shortcomings; but, instead of that, he would praise him twice as much as soon as he found out what was my father's object.

One winter-time, when I was about sixteen, and Gregory nineteen, I was sent by my father on an errand to a place about seven miles distant by the road, but only about four by the Fells. He bade me return by the road, whichever way I took in going, for the evenings closed in early, and were often thick and misty; besides which, old Adam, now paralytic and bedridden, foretold a downfall of snow before long.

I soon got to my journey's end, and soon had done my business; earlier by an hour, I thought, than my father had expected, so I took the decision of the way by which I would return into my own hands, and set off back again over the Fells, just as the first shades of evening began to fall. It looked dark and gloomy enough; but everything was so still that I thought I should have plenty of time to get home before the snow came down.

Off I set at a pretty quick pace. But night came on quicker. The right path was clear enough in the daytime, although at several points two or three exactly similar diverged from the same place; but when there was a good light, the traveller was guided by the sight of distant objects, – a piece of rock, – a fall in the ground – which were quite invisible to me now. I plucked up a brave heart, however, and took what seemed to me the right road. It was wrong, however, and let me whither I knew not, but to some wild boggy moor where the solitude seemed painful, intense, as if never footfall of man had come thither to break the silence.

I tried to shout, – with the dimmest possible hope of being heard – rather to reassure myself by the sound of my own voice; but my voice came husky and short, and yet it dismayed me; it seemed so weird and strange in that noiseless expanse of black darkness. Suddenly the air was filled thick with dusky flakes, my face and hands were wet with snow. It cut me off from the slightest knowledge of where I was, for I lost every idea of the direction from which I had come, so that I could not even retrace my steps; it hemmed me in, thicker, thicker, with a darkness that might be felt. The boggy soil on which I stood quaked under me if I remained long in one place, and yet I dared not move far.

All my youthful hardiness seemed to leave me at once. I was on the point of crying, and only very shame seemed to keep it down. To save myself from shedding tears, I shouted – terrible, wild shouts for bare life they were. I turned sick as I paused to listen; no answering sound came but the unfeeling echoes. Only the noise-less, pitiless snow kept falling thicker, thicker – faster, faster! I was growing numb and sleepy. I tried to move about, but I dared not go far, for fear of the precipices which, I knew, abounded in certain places on the Fells. Now and then, I stood still and shouted again; but my voice was getting choked with tears, as I thought of the desolate, helpless death I was to die, and how little they at home, sitting round the warm, red, bright fire, wotted what was become of me, – and how my poor father would grieve for me – it would surely kill him – it would break his heart, poor old man! Aunt Fanny too – was this to be the end of all her cares for me?

I began to review my life in a strange kind of vivid dream, in which the various scenes of my few boyish years passed before me like visions. In a pang of agony, caused by such remembrance of my short life, I gathered up my strength and called out once more, a long, despairing, wailing cry, to which I had no hope of obtaining any answer, save from the echoes around, dulled as the sound might be by the thickened air.

To my surprise, I heard a cry – almost as long, as wild as mine – so wild that it seemed unearthly, and I almost thought it must be the voice of some of the mocking spirits of the Fells, about whom I had heard so many tales. My heart suddenly began to beat fast and loud. I could not reply for a minute or two. I nearly fancied I had lost the power of utterance.

Just at this moment a dog barked. Was it Lassie's bark – my brother's collie? – an ugly enough brute, with a white, ill-looking face, that my father always kicked whenever he saw it, partly for its own demerits, partly because it belonged to my brother. On such occasions, Gregory would whistle Lassie away, and go off and sit with her in some outhouse.

My father had once or twice been ashamed of himself, when the poor collie had yowled out with the suddenness of the pain, and had relieved himself of his self-reproach by blaming my brother, who, he said, had no notion of training a dog, and was enough to ruin any collie in Christendom with his stupid way of allowing them to lie by the kitchen fire. To all which Gregory would answer nothing, nor even seem to hear, but go on looking absent and moody. Yes! there again! It was Lassie's bark! Now or never! I lifted up my voice and shouted 'Lassie! Lassie! For God's sake, Lassie!'

Another moment, and the great white-faced Lassie was curving and gambolling with delight round my feet and legs, looking, however, up in my face with her intelligent, apprehensive eyes, as if fearing lest I might greet her with a blow, as I had done oftentimes before. But I cried with gladness, as I stooped down and patted her. My mind was sharing in my body's weakness, and I could not reason, but I knew that help was at hand. A grey figure came more and more distinctly out of the thick, close-pressing darkness. It was Gregory wrapped in his maud.[6]

'Oh, Gregory!' said I, and I fell upon his neck, unable to speak another word. He never spoke much,

[6] woollen cloak

and made me no answer for some little time. Then he told me we must move, we must walk for the dear life – we must find our road home, if possible; but we must move or we should be frozen to death.

'Don't you know the way home?' asked I.

'I thought I did when I set out, but I am doubtful now. The snow blinds me, and I am feared that in moving about just now I have lost the right gait homewards.'

He had his shepherd's staff with him, and by dint of plunging it before us at every step we took – clinging close to each other, we went on safely enough, as far as not falling down any of the steep rocks, but it was slow, dreary work. My brother, I saw, was more guided by Lassie and the way she took than anything else, trusting to her instinct. It was too dark to see far before us; but he called her back continually, and noted from what quarter she returned, and shaped our slow steps accordingly. But the tedious motion scarcely kept my very blood from freezing. Every bone, every fibre in my body seemed first to ache, and then to swell, and then to turn numb with the intense cold. My brother bore it better than I, from having been more out upon the hills. He did not speak, except to call Lassie. I strove to be brave, and not complain; but now I felt the deadly fatal sleep stealing over me.

'I can go no farther,' I said, in a drowsy tone. I remember I suddenly became dogged and resolved. Sleep I would, were it only for five minutes. If death were to be the consequence, sleep I would. Gregory stood still. I suppose he recognised the peculiar phase of suffering to which I had been brought by the cold.

'It is of no use,' said he, as if to himself. 'We are no nearer home than we were when we started, as far as I can tell. Our only chance is in Lassie. Here! roll thee in my maud, lad, and lay thee down on this sheltered side of this bit of rock. Creep close under it, lad, and I'll lie by thee, and strive to keep the warmth in us. Stay! hast gotten aught about thee they'll know at home?'

I felt him unkind thus to keep me from slumber, but on his repeating the question, I pulled out my pocket-handkerchief, of some showy pattern, which Aunt Fanny had hemmed for me – Gregory took it, and tied it round Lassie's neck.

'Hie thee, Lassie, hie thee home!' And the white-faced, ill-favoured brute was off like a shot in the darkness. Now I might lie down – now I might sleep. In my drowsy stupor I felt that I was being tenderly covered up by my brother; but what with I neither knew nor cared – I was too dull, too selfish, too numb to think and reason, or I might have known that in that bleak bare place there was naught to wrap me in, save what was taken off another. I was glad enough when he ceased his cares and lay down by me. I took his hand.

'Thou canst not remember, lad, how we lay together thus by our dying mother. She put thy small, wee hand in mine – I reckon she sees us now; and belike we shall soon be with her. Anyhow, God's will be done.'

'Dear Gregory,' I muttered, and crept nearer to him for warmth. He was talking still, and again about our mother, when I fell asleep. In an instant – or so it seemed – there were many voices about me – many faces hovering round me – the sweet luxury of warmth was stealing into every part of me. I was in my own little bed at home. I am thankful to say, my first word was 'Gregory?'

A look passed from one to another – my father's stern old face strove[7] in vain to keep its sternness; his mouth quivered, his eyes filled slowly with unwonted tears.

[7] tried hard

'I would have given him half my land – I would have blessed him as my son, – oh God! I would have knelt at his feet, and asked him to forgive my hardness of heart.'

I heard no more. A whirl came through my brain, catching me back to death. I came slowly to my consciousness, weeks afterwards. My father's hair was white when I recovered, and his hands shook as he looked into my face.

We spoke no more of Gregory. We could not speak of him; but he was strangely in our thoughts. Lassie came and went with never a word of blame; nay, my father would try to stroke her, but she shrank away; and he, as if reproved by the poor dumb beast, would sigh, and be silent and abstracted for a time.

Aunt Fanny – always a talker – told me all. How, on that fatal night, my father, irritated by my prolonged absence, and probably more anxious than he cared to show, had been fierce and imperious,[8] even beyond his wont, to Gregory: had upbraided[9] him with his father's poverty, his own stupidity which made his services good for nothing – for so, in spite of the old shepherd, my father always chose to consider them.

At last, Gregory had risen up, and whistled Lassie out with him – poor Lassie, crouching underneath his chair for fear of a kick or a blow. Some time before, there had been some talk between my father and my aunt respecting my return; and when Aunt Fanny told me all this, she said she fancied that Gregory might have noticed the coming storm, and gone out silently to meet me. Three hours afterwards, when all were running about in wild alarm, not knowing whither to go in search of me – not even missing Gregory, or

[8] tyrannical
[9] criticised

heeding his absence, poor fellow – poor, poor fellow! – Lassie came home, with my handkerchief tied round her neck. They knew and understood, and the whole strength of the farm was turned out to follow her, with wraps, and blankets, and brandy, and everything that could be thought of. I lay in chilly sleep, but still alive, beneath the rock that Lassie guided them to. I was covered over with my brother's plaid, and his thick shepherd's coat was carefully wrapped round my feet. He was in his shirt-sleeves – his arm thrown over me – a quiet smile (he had hardly ever smiled in life) upon his still, cold face.

My father's last words were, 'God forgive me my hardness of heart towards the fatherless child!'

And what marked the depth of his feeling of repentance, perhaps more than all, considering the passionate love he bore my mother, was this: we found a paper of directions after his death, in which he desired that he might lie at the foot of the grave in which, by his desire, poor Gregory had been laid with OUR MOTHER.

Bang, Bang – Who's Dead?

by Jane Gardam

There is an old house in Kent not far from the sea where a little ghost girl plays in the garden. She wears the same clothes winter and summer – long black stockings, a white dress with a pinafore, and her hair flying about without a hat, but she never seems either hot or cold. They say she was a child of the house who was run over at the drive gates, for the road outside is on an upward bend as you come to the gates of The Elms – that's the name of the house, The Elms – and very dangerous. But there were no motor cars when children wore clothes like that and so the story must be rubbish.

No grown person has ever seen the child. Only other children see her. For over fifty years, when children have visited this garden and gone off to play in it, down the avenue of trees, into the walled rose-garden, or down deep under the high dark caves of the polished shrubs where queer things scutter and scrattle about on quick legs and eyes look out at you from round corners, and pheasants send up great alarm calls like rattles, and whirr off out of the wet hard bracken right under your nose, 'Where've you been?' they get asked when they get back to the house.

'Playing with that girl in the garden.'

'What girl? There's no girl here. This house has no children in it.'

'Yes it has. There's a girl in the garden. She can't half run.'

When last year The Elms came up for sale, two parents – the parents of a girl called Fran – looked at each other with a great longing gaze. The Elms.

'We could never afford it.'

'I don't know. It's in poor condition. We might. They daren't ask much for such an overgrown place.'

'All that garden. We'd never be able to manage it. And the house is so far from anywhere.'

'It's mostly woodland. It looks after itself.'

'Don't you believe it. Those elms would all have to come down for a start. They're diseased. There's masses of replanting and clearing to do. And think of the upkeep of that long drive.'

'It's a beautiful house. And not really a huge one.'

'And would you *want* to live in a house with –'

They both looked at Fran who had never heard of the house. 'With what?' she asked.

'Is it haunted?' she asked. She knew things before you ever said them. Almost before you thought of them.

'Of course not,' said her father.

'Yes,' said her mother.

Fran gave a squealing shudder.

'Now you've done it,' said her father. 'No point now in even going to look at it.'

'How is it haunted?' asked Fran.

'It's only the garden,' said her mother. 'And very *nicely* haunted. By a girl about your age in black stockings and a pinafore.'

'What's a pinafore.'

'Apron.'

'*Apron.* How cruddy.'

'She's from the olden days.'

'Fuddy-duddy-cruddy,' said Fran, preening herself about in her tee-shirt and jeans.

After a while though she noticed that her parents

were still rattling on about The Elms. There would be spurts of talks and then long silences. They would stand for ages moving things pointlessly about on the kitchen table, drying up the same plate three times. Gazing out of windows. In the middle of Fran telling them something about her life at school they would say suddenly, 'Rats. I expect it's overrun with rats.'

Or, 'What about the roof?'

Or, 'I expect some millionaire will buy it for a Country Club. Oh, it's far beyond us, you know.'

'When are we going to look at it?' asked Fran after several days of this, and both parents turned to her with faraway eyes.

'I want to see this girl in the garden,' said Fran because it was a bright sunny morning and the radio was playing loud and children not of the olden days were in the street outside, hurling themselves about on bikes and wearing jeans and tee-shirts like her own and shouting out, 'Bang, bang, you're dead.'

'Well, I suppose we could just telephone,' said her mother. 'Make an appointment.'

Then electricity went flying about the kitchen and her father began to sing.

They stopped the car for a moment inside the propped-back iron gates where there stood a rickety table with a box on it labelled 'Entrance Fee. One pound.'

'We don't pay an entrance fee,' said Fran's father. 'We're here on business.'

'When I came here as a child,' said Fran's mother, 'we always threw some money in.'

'Did you often come?'

'Oh, once or twice. Well yes. Quite often. Whenever we had visitors we always brought them to The Elms. We used to tell them about –'

'Oh yes. Ha-ha. The ghost.'

'Well, it was just something to do with people. On a visit. I'd not be surprised if the people in the house made up the ghost just to get people to come.'

The car ground along the silent drive. The drive curved round and round. Along and along. A young deer leapt from one side of it to the other in the green shadow, its eyes like lighted grapes. Water in a pool in front of the house came into view.

The house held light from the water. It was a long, low, creamy coloured house covered with trellis and on the trellis pale wisteria, pale clematis, large papery early roses. A huge man was staring from the ground-floor window.

'Is that the ghost?' asked Fran.

Her father sagely, solemnly parked the car. The air in the garden for a moment seemed to stir, the colours to fade. Fran's mother looked up at the gentle old house.

'Oh – look,' she said, 'It's a portrait. Of a man. He seems to be looking out. It's just a painting, for goodness sake.'

But the face of the long-dead seventeenth-century man eyed the terrace, the semi-circular flight of steps, the family of three looking up at him beside their motor car.

'It's just a painting.'

'Do we ring the bell? At the front door?'

The half-glazed inner front door above the staircase of stone seemed the door of another shadowy world.

'I don't want to go in,' said Fran. 'I'll stay here.'

'Look, if we're going to buy this house,' said her father, 'you must come and look at it.'

'I want to go in the garden,' said Fran. 'Anyone can see the house is going to be all right.'

All three surveyed the pretty house. Along the top floor of it were heavily barred windows.

'They barred the windows long ago,' said Fran's mother, 'to stop the children falling out. The children lived upstairs. Every evening they were allowed to come down and see their parents for half an hour and then they went back up there to bed. It was the custom for children.'

'Did the ghost girl do that?'

'Don't be ridiculous,' said Fran's father.

'But did she?'

'What ghost girl?' said Fran's father. 'Shut up and come and let's look at the house.'

A man and a woman were standing at the end of the hall as the family rang the bell. They were there waiting, looking rather vague and thin. Fran could feel a sadness and anxiety through the glass of the wide, high door, the woman with her gaunt old face just standing; the man blinking.

In the beautiful stone hall at the foot of the stairs the owners and the parents and Fran confronted each other. Then the four grown people advanced with their hands outstretched, like some dance.

'The house has always been in my family,' said the woman. 'For two hundred years.'

'Can I go out?' asked Fran.

'For over fifty years it was the possession of three sisters. My three great-aunts.'

'Mum – can I? I'll stay by the car.'

'They never married. They adored the house. They scarcely ever left it or had people to stay. There were never any children in this house.'

'Mum –'

'*Do*,' said the woman to Fran. 'Do go and look around the garden. Perfectly safe. Far from the road.'

The four adults walked away down the stone passage. A door to the dining-room was opened. 'This,' said the woman, 'is said to be the most beautiful dining-room in Kent.'

'What was that?' asked Fran's mother. 'Where is Fran?'

But Fran seemed happy. All four watched her in her white tee-shirt running across the grass. They watched her through the dining-room window all decorated round with frills and garlands of wisteria. 'What a sweet girl,' said the woman. The man cleared his throat and went wandering away.

'I think it's because there have never been any children in this house that it's in such beautiful condition,' said the woman. 'Nobody has even been unkind to it.'

'I wouldn't say,' said Fran's mother, 'that children were –'

'Oh, but you can tell a house where children have taken charge. Now your dear little girl would never –'

The parents were taken into a room that smelled of rose-petals. A cherry-wood fire was burning although the day was very hot. Most of the fire was soft white ash. Somebody had been doing some needlework. Dogs slept quietly on a rug. 'Oh, Fran would love –' said Fran's mother looking out of the window again. But Fran was not to be seen.

'Big family?' asked the old man suddenly.

'No. Just – Just one daughter, Fran.'

'Big house for just one child.'

'But you said there had never been children in this house.'

'Oh – wouldn't say never. Wouldn't say never.'

Fran had wandered away towards the garden but then

had come in again to the stone hall, where she stopped to look at herself in a long dim glass. There was a blue jar with a lid on a low table, and she lifted the lid and saw a heap of dried rose-petals. The lid dropped back rather hard and wobbled on the jar as if to fall off. 'Children are unkind to houses,' she heard the floating voice of the woman shepherding her parents from one room to another. Fran pulled an unkind face at the jar. She turned a corner of the hall and saw the staircase sweeping upwards and round a corner. On the landing someone seemed to be standing, but then as she looked seemed not to be there after all. 'Oh yes,' she heard the woman's voice, 'oh yes, I suppose so. Lovely for children. The old nurseries should be very adequate. We never go up there.'

'If there are nurseries,' said Fran's father, 'there must once have been children.'

'I suppose so. Once. It's not a thing we ever think about.'

'But if it has always been in your family it must have been inherited by children?'

'Oh cousins. Generally cousins inherited. Quite strange how children have not been actually born here.' Fran, who was sitting outside on the steps now in front of the open door, heard the little group clatter off along the stone pavement to the kitchens and thought, 'Why are they going on about children so?'

She thought, 'When they come back I'll go with them. I'll ask to see that painted man down the passage. I'd rather be with Mum to see him close.'

Silence had fallen. The house behind her was still, the garden in front of her stiller. It was the moment in an English early summer afternoon when there is a pause for sleep. Even the birds stop singing. Tired by their almost non-stop territorial squawks and cheeps and trills since dawn, they declare a truce and sit still upon branches, stand with heads cocked listening, scamper now and then in the bushes across dead leaves. When Fran listened very hard she thought she could just hear the swish of the road, or perhaps the sea. The smell of the early roses was very strong. Somewhere upstairs a window was opened and a light voice came and went as people moved from room to room. 'Must have gone up the back stairs,' Fran thought and leaned her head against the fluted column of the portico. It was strange. She felt she knew what the house looked like upstairs. Had she been upstairs yet or was she still thinking of going? Going. Going to sleep. Silly.

She jumped up and said, 'You can't catch me. Bang, bang – you're dead.'

She didn't know what she meant by it so she said it again out loud. 'Bang, bang. You're dead.'

She looked at the garden, all the way round from her left to her right. Nothing stirred. Not from the point where a high wall stood with a flint arch in it, not on the circular terrace with the round pond, not in the circle of green with the round gap in it where the courtyard opened to the long drive, and where their car was standing. The car made her feel safe.

Slowly round went her look, right across to where the stone urns on the right showed a mossy path behind them. Along the path, out of the shadow of the house, the sun was blazing and you could see bright flowers.

Fran walked to the other side of the round pond and looked up at the house from the courtyard and saw the portrait again looking at her. It must be hanging in a very narrow passage, she thought, to be so near to the glass. The man was in some sort of uniform. You could see gold on his shoulders and lace on his cuffs. You could see long curls falling over his shoulders. Fancy soldiers with long curls hanging over their uniform! Think of the dandruff.

'Olden days,' said Fran. 'Bang, bang, you're dead,' and she set off at a run between the stone urns and into the flower garden. 'I'll run right round the house,' she thought. 'I'll run like mad. Then I'll say I've been all round the garden by myself, and not seen the ghost.'

She ran like the wind all round, leaping the flower-beds, tearing along a showering rose-border, here and there, up and down, flying through another door in a stone wall among greenhouses and sheds and old stables, out again past a rose-red dove-house with the doves like fat pearls set in some of the little holes, and others stepping about the grass. Non-stop, non-stop she ran, across the lawn, right turn through a yew hedge, through the flint arch at last and back to the courtyard. 'Oh yes,' she would say to her friends on their bikes. 'I did. I've been there. I've been all round the garden by myself and I didn't see a living soul.'

'A *living* soul.'

'I didn't see any ghost. Never even thought of one.'

'You're brave, Fran. I'd never be brave like that. Are your parents going to buy the house?'

'Don't suppose so. It's very boring. They've never had any children in it. Like an old-folks home. Not even haunted.'

Picking a draggle of purple wisteria off the courtyard wall – and pulling rather a big trail of it down as she did so – Fran began to do the next brave thing: to *walk* round the house. Slowly. She pulled a few petals off the wisteria and gave a carefree sort of wave at the portrait in the window. In front of it, looking out of the window, stood a little girl.

Then she was gone.

For less than a flick of a second Fran went cold round the back of the neck. Then hot.

Then she realised she must be going loopy. The girl hadn't been in a pinafore and frilly dress and long loose hair. She'd been in a white tee-shirt like Fran's own. She had been Fran's own reflection for a moment in the glass of the portrait.

'Stupid. Loopy,' said Fran, picking off petals and scattering them down the mossy path, then along the rosy flag-stones of the rose garden. Her heart was beating very hard. It was almost pleasant, the fright and then the relief coming so close together.

'Well, I thought I saw the ghost but it was only myself reflected in a window,' she'd say to the friends in the road at home.

'Oh Fran, you are brave.'

'How d'you know it was you? Did you see its face? Everyone wears tee-shirts.'

'Oh, I expect it was me all right. They said there'd never been any children in the house.'

'What a cruddy house. I'll bet it's not true. I'll bet there's a girl they're keeping in there somewhere. Behind those bars. I bet she's being imprisoned. I bet they're kidnappers.'

'They wouldn't be showing people over the house and trying to sell it if they were kidnappers. Not while the kidnapping was actually going on, anyway. No, you can tell –' Fran was explaining away, pulling off the petals. 'There wasn't anyone there but me.' She looked up at the windows in the stable-block she was passing. They were partly covered with creeper, but one of them stood open and a girl in a tee-shirt was sitting in it, watching Fran.

This time she didn't vanish. Her shiny short hair and

white shirt shone out clear. Across her humped-up knees lay a comic. She was very much the present day.

'It's you again,' she said.

She was so ordinary that Fran's heart did not begin to thump at all. She thought, 'It must be the gardener's daughter. They must live over the stables and she's just been in the house. I'll bet she wasn't meant to. That's why she ducked away.'

'I saw you in the house,' Fran said. 'I thought you were a reflection of me.'

'Reflection?'

'In the picture.'

The girl looked disdainful. 'When you've been in the house as long as I have,' she said, 'let's hope you'll know a bit more. Oil paintings don't give off reflections. They're not covered in glass.'

'We won't be keeping the oil paintings,' said Fran grandly. 'I'm not interested in things like that.'

'I wasn't at first,' said the girl. 'D'you want to come up? You can climb over the creeper if you like. It's cool up here.'

'No thanks. We'll have to go soon. They'll wonder where I am when they see I'm not waiting by the car.'

'Car?' said the girl. 'Did you come in a car?'

'Of course we came in a car.' She felt furious suddenly. The girl was looking at her oddly, maybe as if she wasn't rich enough to have a car. Just because she lived at The Elms. And she was only the gardener's daughter anyway. Who did she think she was?

'Well take care on the turn-out to the road then. It's a dangerous curve. It's much too hot to go driving today.'

'I'm not hot,' said Fran.

'You ought to be,' said the girl in the tee-shirt, 'with all that hair and those awful black stockings.'

The Signalman

by Charles Dickens

'Halloa! Below there!'

When he heard a voice thus calling to him, he was standing at the door of his box, with a flag in his hand, furled round its short pole. One would have thought, considering the nature of the ground, that he could not have doubted from what quarter the voice came; but, instead of looking up to where I stood on the top of the steep cutting nearly over his head, he turned himself about and looked down the Line. There was something remarkable in his manner of doing so, though I could not have said for my life, what. But, I know it was remarkable enough to attract my notice, even though his figure was foreshortened and shadowed, down in the deep trench, and mine was high above him, so steeped in the glow of an angry sunset that I had shaded my eyes with my hand before I saw him at all.

'Halloa! Below!'

From looking down the Line, he turned himself about again, and, raising his eyes, saw my figure high above him.

'Is there any path by which I can come down and speak to you?'

He looked up at me without replying, and I looked down at him without pressing him too soon with a repetition of my idle question. Just then, there came a vague vibration in the earth and air, quickly changing into a violent pulsation, and an oncoming rush that caused me to start back, as though it had force to draw me down. When such vapour as rose to my height from this rapid train, had passed me and was skimming away over the landscape, I looked down again, and saw him re-furling the flag he had shown while the train went by.

I repeated my inquiry. After a pause, during which he seemed to regard me with fixed attention, he motioned with his rolled-up flag towards a point on my level, some two or three hundred yards distant. I called down to him, 'All right!' and made for that point. There, by dint of looking closely about me, I found a rough zig-zag descending path notched out: which I followed.

The cutting was extremely deep, and unusually precipitate.[1] It was made through a clammy stone that became oozier and wetter as I went down. For these reasons, I found the way long enough to give me time to recall a singular air of reluctance or compulsion with which he had pointed out the path.

When I came down low enough upon the zig-zag descent, to see him again, I saw that he was standing between the rails on the way by which the train had lately passed, in an attitude as if he were waiting for me to appear. He had his left hand at his chin, and that left elbow rested on his right hand crossed over his breast. His attitude was one of such expectation and watchfulness, that I stopped a moment, wondering at it.

I resumed my downward way, and, stepping out upon the level of the railroad and drawing nearer to him, saw that he was a dark sallow man, with a dark beard and rather heavy eyebrows. His post was in as solitary and dismal a place as ever I saw. On either side, a dripping-wet wall of jagged stone, excluding all view but a strip of sky; the perspective one way, only a crooked

[1] steep

prolongation of this great dungeon; the shorter perspective in the other direction, terminating in a gloomy red light, and the gloomier entrance to a black tunnel, in whose massive architecture there was a barbarous, depressing, and forbidding air. So little sunlight ever found its way to this spot, that it had an earthy deadly smell; and so much cold wind rushed through it, that it struck chill to me, as if I had left the natural world.

Before he stirred, I was near enough to him to have touched him. Not even then removing his eyes from mine, he stepped back one step, and lifted his hand.

This was a lonesome post to occupy (I said), and it had riveted my attention when I looked down from up yonder. A visitor was a rarity, I should suppose; not an unwelcome rarity, I hoped? In me, he merely saw a man who had been shut up within narrow limits all his life, and who, being at last set free, had a newly-awakened interest in these great works. To such purpose I spoke to him; but I am far from sure of the terms I used, for, besides that I am not happy in opening any conversation, there was something in the man that daunted me.[2]

He directed a most curious look towards the red light near the tunnel's mouth, and looked all about it, as if something were missing from it, and then looked at me.

That light was part of his charge? Was it not?

He answered in a low voice: 'Don't you know it is?'

The monstrous thought came into my mind as I perused the fixed eyes and the saturnine face, that this was a spirit, not a man. I have speculated since, whether there may have been infection in his mind.

In my turn, I stepped back. But in making the action, I detected in his eyes some latent fear of me. This put the monstrous thought to flight.

[2] put me off

'You look at me,' I said, forcing a smile, 'as if you had a dread of me.'

'I was doubtful,' he returned, 'whether I had seen you before.'

'Where?'

He pointed to the red light he had looked at.

'There?' I said.

Intently watchful of me, he replied (but without sound), Yes.

'My good fellow, what should I do there? However, be that as it may, I never was there, you may swear.'

'I think I may,' he rejoined. 'Yes. I am sure I may.'

His manner cleared, like my own. He replied to my remarks with readiness, and in well-chosen words. Had he much to do there? Yes; that was to say, he had enough responsibility to bear; but exactness and watchfulness were what was required of him, and of actual work – manual labour – he had next to none. To change that signal, to trim those lights, and to turn this iron handle now and then, was all he had to do under that head. Regarding those many long and lonely hours of which I seemed to make so much, he could only say that the routine of his life had shaped itself into that form, and he had grown used to it. He had taught himself a language down here – if only to know it by sight, and to have formed his own crude ideas of its pronunciation, could be called learning it. He had also worked at fractions and decimals, and tried a little algebra; but he was, and had been as a boy, a poor hand at figures. Was it necessary for him when on duty, always to remain in that channel of damp air, and could he never rise into the sunshine from between those high stone walls? Why, that depended upon times and circumstances. Under some conditions there would be less upon the Line than under others, and the same held good as to certain hours of the day and night. In bright weather, he did choose occasions for getting a little above those lower shadows; but, being at all times liable to be called by his electric bell, and at such times listening for it with redoubled anxiety, the relief was less than I would suppose.

He took me into his box, where there was a fire, a desk for an official book in which he had to make certain entries, a telegraphic instrument with its dial face and needles, and the little bell of which he had spoken. On my trusting that he would excuse the remark that he had been well educated, and (I hoped I might say without offence), perhaps educated above that station, he observed that instances of slight incongruity[3] in such-wise would rarely be found wanting among large bodies of men; that he had heard it was so in workhouses, in the police force, even in that last desperate resource, the army; and that he knew it was so, more or less, in any great railway staff. He had been, when young (if I could believe it, sitting in that hut; he scarcely could), a student of natural philosophy, and had attended lectures; but he had run wild, misused his opportunities, gone down, and never risen again. He had no complaint to offer about that. He had made his bed, and he lay upon it. It was far too late to make another.

All that I have here condensed, he said in a quiet manner, with his grave dark regards divided between me and the fire. He threw in the word 'Sir,' from time to time, and especially when he referred to his youth: as though to request me to understand that he claimed to be nothing but what I found him. He was several times interrupted by the little bell, and had to read off

[3] unexpectedness

messages, and send replies. Once, he had to stand without the door, and display a flag as a train passed, and make some verbal communication to the driver. In the discharge of his duties I observed him to be remarkably exact and vigilant, breaking off his discourse at a syllable, and remaining silent until what he had to do was done.

In a word, I should have set this man down as one of the safest of men to be employed in that capacity, but for the circumstance that while he was speaking to me he twice broke off with a fallen colour, turned his face towards the little bell when it did NOT ring, opened the door of the hut (which was kept shut to exclude the unhealthy damp), and looked out towards the red light near the mouth of the tunnel. On both of those occasions, he came back to the fire with the inexplicable air upon him which I had remarked, without being able to define, when we were so far asunder.

Said I when I rose to leave him: 'You almost make me think that I have met with a contented man.'

(I am afraid I must acknowledge that I said it to lead him on.)

'I believe I used to be so,' he rejoined, in the low voice in which he had first spoken; 'but I am troubled, sir, I am troubled.'

He would have recalled the words if he could. He had said them, however, and I took them up quickly.

'With what? What is your trouble?'

'It is very difficult to impart, sir. It is very, very difficult to speak of. If ever you make me another visit, I will try to tell you.'

'But I expressly intend to make you another visit. Say, when shall it be?'

'I go off early in the morning, and I shall be on again at ten tomorrow night, sir.'

'I will come at eleven.'

He thanked me, and went out at the door with me. 'I'll show my white light, sir,' he said, in his peculiar low voice, 'till you have found the way up. When you have found it, don't call out! And when you are at the top, don't call out!'

His manner seemed to make the place strike colder to me, but I said no more than 'Very well.'

'And when you come down tomorrow night, don't call out! Let me ask you a parting question. What made you cry "Halloa! Below there!" tonight?'

'Heaven knows,' said I. 'I cried something to that effect –'

'Not to that effect, sir. Those were the very words. I know them well.'

'Admit those were the very words. I said them, no doubt, because I saw you below.'

'For no other reason?'

'What other reason could I possibly have!'

'You have no feeling that they were conveyed to you in any supernatural way?'

'No.'

He wished me good night, and held up his light. I walked by the side of the down Line of rails (with a very disagreeable sensation of a train coming behind me), until I found the path. It was easier to mount than to descend, and I got back to my inn without any adventure.

Punctual to my appointment, I placed my foot on the first notch of the zig-zag next night, as the distant clocks were striking eleven. He was waiting for me at the bottom, with his white light on. 'I have not called out,' I said, when we came close together; 'may I speak now?' 'By all means, sir.' 'Good night then, and here's my hand.' 'Good night, sir, and here's mine.' With that, we walked side by side to his box, entered it, closed the door, and sat down by the fire.

'I have made up my mind, sir,' he began, bending forward as soon as we were seated, and speaking in a tone but a little above a whisper, 'that you shall not have to ask me twice what troubles me. I took you for someone else yesterday evening. That troubles me.'

'That mistake?'

'No. That someone else.'

'Who is it?'

'I don't know.'

'Like me?'

'I don't know. I never saw the face. The left arm is across the face, and the right arm is waved. Violently waved. This way.'

I followed his action with my eyes, and it was the action of an arm gesticulating with the utmost passion and vehemence: 'For God's sake clear the way!'

'One moonlight night,' said the man, 'I was sitting here, when I heard a voice cry "Halloa! Below there!" I started up, looked from that door, and saw this Someone else standing by the red light near the tunnel, waving as I just now showed you. The voice seemed hoarse with shouting, and it cried, "Look out! Look out!" And then again "Halloa! Below there! Look out!" I caught up my lamp, turned it on red, and ran towards the figure, calling, "What's wrong? What has happened? Where?" It stood just outside the blackness of the tunnel. I advanced so close upon it that I wondered at its keeping the sleeve across its eyes. I ran right up at it, and had my hand stretched out to pull the sleeve away, when it was gone.'

'Into the tunnel,' said I.

'No. I ran on into the tunnel, five hundred yards. I stopped and held my lamp above my head, and saw the figures of the measured distance, and saw the wet stains stealing down the walls and trickling through the arch. I ran out again, faster than I had run in (for I had a mortal abhorrence of the place upon me), and I looked all round the red light with my own red light, and I went up the iron ladder to the gallery atop of it, and I came down again, and ran back here. I telegraphed both ways: "An alarm has been given. Is anything wrong?" The answer came back, both ways: "All well."'

Resisting the slow touch of a frozen finger tracing out my spine, I showed him how that this figure must be a deception of his sense of sight, and how that figures, originating in disease of the delicate nerves that minister to the functions of the eye, were known to have often troubled patients, some of whom had become conscious of the nature of their affliction, and had even proved it by experiments upon themselves. 'As to an imaginary cry,' said I, 'do but listen for a moment to the wind in this unnatural valley while we speak so low, and to the wild harp it makes of the telegraph wires!'

That was all very well, he returned, after we had sat listening for a while and he ought to know something of the wind and the wires, he who so often passed long winter nights there, alone and watching. But he would beg to remark that he had not finished.

I asked his pardon, and he slowly added these words, touching my arm:

'Within six hours after the Appearance, the memorable accident on this Line happened, and within ten hours the dead and wounded were brought along through the tunnel over the spot where the figure had stood.'

A disagreeable shudder crept over me, but I did my best against it. It was not to be denied, I rejoined, that this was a remarkable coincidence, calculated deeply to impress his mind. But, it was unquestionable that remarkable coincidences did continually occur, and they must be taken into account in dealing with such a subject. Though to be sure I must admit, I added (for I thought I saw that he was going to bring the objection to bear upon me), men of common sense did not allow much for coincidences in making the ordinary calculations of life.

He again begged to remark that he had not finished.

I again begged his pardon for being betrayed into interruptions.

'This,' he said, again laying his hand upon my arm, and glancing over his shoulder with hollow eyes, 'was just a year ago. Six or seven months passed, and I had recovered from the surprise and shock, when one morning, as the day was breaking, I, standing at that door, looked towards the red light, and saw the spectre again.' He stopped, with a fixed look at me.

'Did it cry out?'

'No. It was silent.'

'Did it wave its arm?'

'No. It leaned against the shaft of the light, with both hands before the face. Like this.'

Once more, I followed his action with my eyes. It was an action of mourning. I have seen such an attitude in stone figures on tombs.

'Did you go up to it?'

'I came in and sat down, partly to collect my thoughts, partly because it had turned me faint. When I went to the door again, daylight was above me, and the ghost was gone.'

'But nothing followed? Nothing came of this?'

He touched me on the arm with his forefinger twice or thrice, giving a ghastly nod each time:

'That very day, as a train came out of the tunnel, I noticed, at a carriage window on my side, what looked like a confusion of hands and heads, and something waved. I saw it, just in time to signal the driver, Stop! He shut off, and put his brake on, but the train drifted past here a hundred and fifty yards or more. I ran after it, and, as I went along, heard terrible screams and cries. A beautiful young lady had died instantaneously in one of the compartments, and was brought in here, and laid down on this floor between us.'

Involuntarily, I pushed my chair back, as I looked from the boards at which he pointed, to himself.

'True, sir. True. Precisely as it happened, so I tell it you.'

I could think of nothing to say, to any purpose, and my mouth was very dry. The wind and the wires took up the story with a long lamenting wail.

He resumed. 'Now, sir, mark this, and judge how my mind is troubled. The spectre came back, a week ago. Ever since, it has been there, now and again, by fits and starts.'

'At the light?'

'At the Danger-light.'

'What does it seem to do?'

He repeated, if possible with increased passion and vehemence, that former gesticulation of 'For God's sake clear the way!'

Then, he went on. 'I have no peace or rest for it. It calls to me, for many minutes together, in an agonised manner, "Below there! Look out! Look out!" It stands waving to me. It rings my little bell —'

I caught at that. 'Did it ring your bell yesterday evening when I was here, and you went to the door?'

'Twice.'

'Why, see,' said I, 'how your imagination misleads you.

My eyes were on the bell, and my ears were open to the bell, and if I am a living man, it did NOT ring at those times. No, nor at any other time, except when it was rung in the natural course of physical things by the station communicating with you.'

He shook his head. 'I have never made a mistake as to that, yet, sir. I have never confused the spectre's ring with the man's. The ghost's ring is a strange vibration in the bell that it derives from nothing else, and I have not asserted that the bell stirs to the eye. I don't wonder that you failed to hear it. But *I* heard it.'

'And did the spectre seem to be there, when you looked out?'

'It WAS there.'

'Both times?'

He repeated firmly: 'Both times.'

'Will you come to the door with me, and look for it now?'

He bit his under-lip as though he were somewhat unwilling, but arose. I opened the door, and stood on the step, while he stood in the doorway. There, was the Danger-light. There, was the dismal mouth of the tunnel. There, were the high wet stone walls of the cutting. There, were the stars above them.

'Do you see it?' I asked him, taking particular note of his face. His eyes were prominent and strained; but not very much more so, perhaps, than my own had been when I had directed them earnestly towards the same spot.

'No,' he answered. 'It is not there.'

'Agreed,' said I.

We went in again, shut the door, and resumed our seats. I was thinking how best to improve this advantage, if it might be called one, when he took up the conversation in such a matter of course way, so assuming that there could be no serious question of fact between us, that I felt myself in the weakest of positions.

'By this time you will fully understand, sir,' he said, 'that what troubles me so dreadfully, is the question, What does the spectre mean?'

I was not sure, I told him, that I did fully understand.

'What is its warning against?' he said, ruminating, with his eyes on the fire, and only by times turning them on me. 'What is the danger? Where is the danger? There is danger overhanging, somewhere on the Line. Some dreadful calamity will happen. It is not to be doubted this third time, after what has gone before. But surely this is a cruel haunting of *me*. What can *I* do!'

He pulled out his handkerchief, and wiped the drops from his heated forehead.

'If I telegraph Danger, on either side of me, or on both, I can give no reason for it,' he went on, wiping the palms of his hands. 'I should get into trouble, and do no good. They would think I was mad. This is the way it would work: Message: "Danger! Take care!" Answer: "What Danger? Where?" Message: "Don't know. But for God's sake take care!" They would displace me. What else could they do?'

His pain of mind was most pitiable to see. It was the mental torture of a conscientious man, oppressed beyond endurance by an unintelligible responsibility involving life.

'When it first stood under the Danger-light,' he went on, putting his dark hair back from his head, and drawing his hands outward across and across his temples in an extremity of feverish distress, 'why not tell me where that accident was to happen – if it must happen? Why not tell me how it could be averted – if it could have been averted? When on its second coming it hid its face, why not tell me instead: "She is going to die. Let them keep her at home"? If it came, on those two occasions, only to show me that its warnings were true, and so to prepare me for the third, why not warn me plainly now? And I, Lord help me! A mere poor signalman on this solitary station! Why not go to somebody with credit to be believed, and power to act!'

When I saw him in this state, I saw that for the poor man's sake, as well as for the public safety, what I had to do for the time was, to compose his mind. Therefore, setting aside all question of reality or unreality between us, I represented to him that whoever thoroughly discharged his duty, must do well, and that at least it was his comfort that he understood his duty, though he did not understand these confounding Appearances. In this effort I succeeded far better than in the attempt to reason him out of his conviction. He became calm; the occupations incidental to his post as the night advanced, began to make larger demands on his attention; and I left him at two in the morning. I had offered to stay through the night, but he would not hear of it.

That I more than once looked back at the red light as I ascended the pathway, that I did not like the red light, and that I should have slept but poorly if my bed had been under it, I see no reason to conceal. Nor, did I like the two sequences of the accident and the dead girl. I see no reason to conceal that, either.

But, what ran most in my thoughts was the consideration how ought I to act, having become the recipient of this disclosure? I had proved the man to be intelligent, vigilant, painstaking, and exact; but how long might he remain so, in his state of mind? Though in a subordinate position, still he held a most important trust, and would I (for instance) like to stake my own life on the chances of his continuing to execute it with precision?

Unable to overcome a feeling that there would be something treacherous in my communicating what he had told me, to his superiors in the Company, without first being plain with himself and proposing a middle course to him, I ultimately resolved to offer to accompany him (otherwise keeping his secret for the present) to the wisest medical practitioner we could hear of in those parts, and to take his opinion. A change in his time of duty would come round next night, he had apprised me, and he would be off an hour or two after sunrise, and on again soon after sunset. I had appointed to return accordingly.

Next evening was a lovely evening, and I walked out early to enjoy it. The sun was not yet quite down when I traversed the field-path near the top of the deep cutting. I would extend my walk for an hour, I said to myself, half an hour on and half an hour back, and it would then be time to go to my signalman's box.

Before pursuing my stroll, I stepped to the brink, and mechanically looked down, from the point from which I had first seen him. I cannot describe the thrill that seized upon me, when, close at the mouth of the tunnel, I saw the appearance of a man, with his left sleeve across his eyes, passionately waving his right arm.

The nameless horror that oppressed me, passed in a moment, for in a moment I saw that this appearance of a man was a man indeed, and that there was a little group of other men standing at a short distance, to whom he seemed to be rehearsing the gesture he made. The Danger-light was not yet lighted. Against its shaft, a little low hut, entirely new to me, had been made of some wooden supports and tarpaulin. It looked no bigger than a bed.

With an irresistible sense that something was wrong – with a flashing self-reproachful fear that fatal mischief had come of my leaving the man there, and causing no one to be sent to overlook or correct what he did – I descended the notched path with all the speed I could make.

'What is the matter?' I asked the men.

'Signalman killed this morning, sir.'

'Not the man belonging to that box?'

'Yes, sir.'

'Not the man I know?'

'You will recognise him, sir, if you knew him,' said the man who spoke for the others, solemnly uncovering his own head and raising an end of the tarpaulin, 'for his face is quite composed.'

'O! how did this happen, how did this happen?' I asked, turning from one to another as the hut closed in again.

'He was cut down by an engine, sir. No man in England knew his work better. But somehow he was not clear of the outer rail. It was just at broad day. He had struck the light, and had the lamp in his hand. As the engine came out of the tunnel, his back was towards her, and she cut him down. That man drove her, and was showing how it happened. Show the gentleman, Tom.'

The man, who wore a rough dark dress, stepped back to his former place at the mouth of the tunnel:

'Coming round the curve in the tunnel, sir,' he said, 'I saw him at the end, like as if I saw him down a perspective-glass. There was no time to check speed, and I knew him to be very careful. As he didn't seem to take heed of the whistle, I shut it off when we were running down upon him, and called to him as loud as I could call.'

'What did you say?'

'I said, Below there! Look out! Look out! For God's sake clear the way!'

I started.

'Ah! it was a dreadful time, sir. I never left off calling to him. I put this arm before my eyes, not to see, and I waved this arm to the last; but it was no use.'

Without prolonging the narrative to dwell on any one of its curious circumstances more than on any other, I may, in closing it, point out the coincidence that the warning of the Engine-Driver included, not only the words which the unfortunate Signalman had repeated to me as haunting him, but also the words which I myself – not he – had attached, and that only in my own mind, to the gesticulation[4] he had imitated.

[4] movement of the arm

Activities

A Lesson on a Tortoise

1 As you read the story, make a list of ways in which the school is different from your own – in organisation, groupings, teacher behaviour, atmosphere, relationships, and so on. What similarities are there?

2 What impression do you get of the narrator's attitude to his pupils? Is he: affectionate, dismissive, neutral, eager to please, remote? Choose the word or phrase which fits best, and find evidence from the story to support your viewpoint.

3 D. H. Lawrence emphasises the atmosphere in the classroom. Do you think a student might describe it differently? Imagine being a pupil in the class, the tortoise in front of you, teacher nearby. Write a descriptive paragraph capturing the atmosphere of that Friday afternoon classroom.

4 Why is the teacher so angry about the missing equipment? Would you react in the way he does? Interview him about his response. Does he regret his behaviour at the end of the day? Should he have coped differently with the situation?

5 'But you pick on us – you start on us,' claims one of the boys. Is there any evidence for this in the story?

Coursework

6 The teacher could have been more ruthless in his determination to get the truth out of Ségar about the theft of the rubbers; instead he leaves it. Write an alternative ending to the story in which he cross-examines the pupil more thoroughly about what happened.

The Raffle

1 The pupils at this school clearly have mixed feelings about the character of Mr Hinds. What do they like about him? What do they dislike? Make a list of his positive and negative features.

2 Vidiadhar knows that he is Mr Hinds's favourite, and this worries him. What is Mr Hinds's view? What does he like about Vidiadhar, and how has his attitude changed by the end of the story? Write a monologue showing us the 'before' and 'after' attitudes of Mr Hinds to his 'favourite'.

3 What are Vidiadhar's mother's objections to the goat – its smell, the cost, the inconvenience . . .? Imagine her speaking aloud about her feelings. Role-play or write down what she says.

4 One typical ingredient of a short story is establishing the setting without using too much description. Think of the key scenes in this story by V. S. Naipaul – the school, Vidiadhar's house. How do you visualise them? What are they like? Which details from the writer's style are your impressions based on? For each important setting, make a list of your impressions, and then compare what you have said with someone else in your group.

Coursework

5 Vidiadhar stops going to school at the end of the story.
Why, do you think? Isn't he overreacting? Or do you agree
with him? Imagine a letter he might write to Mr Hinds
explaining why he is so upset, and how his feelings have
changed.

Next Term, We'll Mash You

1 Before reading, look at the unusual title of this story. Make
some guesses as to what it will be about.

2 Look again at the first paragraph of the story. What is going
through the boy's mind at this point? What is he seeing?
What is he thinking? How does he feel? Write a one-
paragraph monologue to show what is happening inside
the boy's mind as he sits in his parents' car, approaching
the school.

3 Imagine the mother explaining later that day why she
chose this school for her son. What reasons would she give?
Role-play or write down a conversation – dominated by the
mother – in which she talks to a friend about what so
impressed her at the school.

4 What clues does Penelope Lively give us about the
snobbery of the parents?

5 Charles's parents obviously like the headmaster and his
wife. What clues can you find in the story to suggest that
they are not all they seem? Aren't they, in fact, quietly
menacing?

Coursework

6 Imagine Charles's diary at the end of that first visit to the school. It is bound to be full of panic and frustration. What does he write? Does he decide to do anything – talk to his parents, for example – or simply accept their decision? Write his diary entry, recalling the grim details of the day from his point of view.

7 Continue the story, starting with Charles's first day at the new school.

Social and historical contexts

- What clues are there in the stories by D. H. Lawrence, V. S. Naipaul and Penelope Lively about when they were written and what society was like then? Look at references to people and places, technology, clothes, behaviour, expectations and conventions. Look at the language used in each story – does any of it feel rooted in a specific period? Make discussion notes on the way the stories compare and contrast in this way, and on similarities and differences with our own time.

Comparisons

- Compare the teachers and pupils in each text – how are they similar and how do they differ?

- How are the different stories told? Which uses first-person narrative (I); which uses third-person mode (she/he)? What effect does this have? Which is most descriptive? Which did you find most enjoyable?

Through the Tunnel

1 Look more closely at the first paragraph of this story by Doris Lessing. What range of emotions are going through Jerry's mind – towards his mother, about wanting to escape? Find two quotations to sum up his mixed feelings.

2 In reply to Jerry's request to go to the bay alone, his mother says, 'Of course, Jerry.' Yet she goes 'worrying off to her beach'. But what is she really thinking at this point? Write a one- or two-paragraph monologue which explores her feelings of worry, loss and, perhaps, guilt.

3 'To be with them, of them, was a craving that filled his whole body.' What is it about the foreign boys that so fascinates Jerry? Why does he so desperately want to be like them? What do they have that he lacks?

4 The story has charted Jerry's obsession with swimming through the tunnel. Yet the last sentence says, 'It was no longer of the least importance to go to the bay.' Why not? Hot-seat Jerry about his changed emotions.

Coursework

5 After his first visit to the bay, Jerry has changed emotionally, and perhaps even physically. What does his mother notice about him? What would she write in that evening's holiday diary? Use some dialogue from the story itself and explore her feelings. You might start with Jerry's demand: 'I want some swimming goggles.'

6 Think about the end of the holiday. What has Jerry learnt? How is he different? Imagine that some years later he looks back on the vacation as a kind of turning-point in his life. What would he say about it? Write his account.

The Voyage

1 What have you learnt about the character of Fenella by the end of the first page? What is she like – how old, her appearance, thoughts, feelings . . .? Make a list of ideas.

2 On page 36 Fenella is surprised to see her father take off his hat. Discuss why she might be surprised. Think also about what we have learnt about her relationship with her father so far. Are they close to one another, do you think? What evidence is there in the text?

3 What do you think is the grandmother's attitude to Fenella? Is she also feeling uncomfortable? Or is sympathy her main emotion? Interview Grandma about her feelings at this point.

4 Discuss what you think the ending of this story by Katherine Mansfield means.

Coursework

5 Look at page 39: 'It was like being shut up in a box with Grandma.' Imagine Fenella's thoughts at this point about her grandmother. How well does she know her? What feels familiar to her and what alien? What is going on inside Fenella's mind? Write a monologue giving an insight.

6 What happens next? Write the next stage of the story, as Fenella adjusts to a new life at her grandparents' home.

The Elephant Man

1 Read the first five pages of this story by Susan Hill and, in particular, the descriptions of Nanny Fawcett. 'Above all, [William] learned that most of the trouble in the world, and all the troubles of women, could be laid at the door of men.' What impressions have you gained of Nanny Fawcett and her attitudes at this early stage in the story? Find some other quotations which seem to sum up her view of the world.

2 When William meets the strange man in the raincoat (page 54) he feels 'uneasy, not liking him to be there'. Interview William to find out more about his impressions of the man.

3 Why do you think Nanny Fawcett is so keen for William to go to the party? Why is William so upset by it?

Coursework

4 By the end of the story, William feels that the world has changed horribly. Imagine his diary in which he writes about how things are different. Use the last paragraph of the story as your starting-point.

Social and historical contexts

- What clues are there in the stories by Doris Lessing, Katherine Mansfield and Susan Hill about when they were written and what society was like then? Look at references to people and places, technology, clothes, behaviour, expectations and conventions. Look at the language used in each story – does any of it feel rooted in a specific period? Make discussion notes on the way the stories compare and contrast in this way, and on similarities and differences with our own time.

Comparisons

- What similarities and differences can you detect in the relationships between older people and young people in these three stories?

- Compare the opening paragraphs of the three stories. How do their styles differ? What differences are there in the words used and the structure?

- One story is about a young girl, the others about young boys. Discuss how the stories would work if the genders in each were reversed.

The Case for the Defence

1 The story is written in the first-person mode (I . . .), and yet the narrator plays no part in it. How would it be different if written simply as she/he? Try rewriting the first paragraph of this story by Graham Greene from a different point of view and compare the effect of your opening paragraph with a friend's.

2 What seem to be the facts of the case? Make a list.

3 The story has a fairly chilling ending. Do you think it would have been better if Mrs Salmon had never reported the crime and gone to court? Interview or hot-seat her about her feelings at the end of the trial.

Coursework

4 Imagine the reaction the trial would have in the community. Write the headline and main story for the front page of the local newspaper. Aim to write around 200 words.

5 What do you think happens next? Continue the story.

The Tell-Tale Heart

1 Reread the first two paragraphs of this story by Edgar Allan Poe and make a list of five points you pick up about the character of the narrator.

2 Imagine you are a doctor or psychiatrist listening to this monologue. What do you make of the narrator? He starts by saying he is not mad, but how do you explain his behaviour? Write a 150-word case study of the person who tells this grim story.

3 Prior to his death, what was the old man's attitude to his murderer? Were they related? Was the killer a lodger? Why didn't the old man keep his door locked? Explore the background to the story.

Coursework

4 The police arrive and show great patience and sense of calm. Do they suspect what has happened from the start? Imagine you are one of the police officers. Think back to your arrival at the house and describe the events from your point of view. Focus in particular on the behaviour of the narrator.

5 What clues can you find as to the age of the story? Does it feel at least 100 years old? Why or why not?

Social and historical contexts

- What clues are there in the stories by Graham Greene and Edgar Allan Poe about when they were written and what society was like then? Look at references to people and places, technology, clothes, behaviour, expectations and conventions. Look at the language used in each story – does any of it feel rooted in a specific period? Make discussion notes on the way the stories compare and contrast in this way, and on similarities and differences with our own time.

Comparisons

- Compare the two 'villains' in the stories. What similarities and differences do you notice?
- Which writer seems more hostile towards his villain? Which is more sympathetic? Find evidence to support your answer.
- Which story has:
  more description?
  more suspense?
  more originality?
  the more gripping ending?
  the livelier style?
- Which do you most enjoy? Why?

The Wounded Cormorant

1 Stop at the end of the first paragraph. What kind of story do you predict that this will be? What do you think is going to happen?

2 'O'Flaherty writes about the birds as if they were almost human,' says one reader. Do you agree? Find evidence to support or disprove this theory.

3 Which of these comments best summarises the 'message' of the story?

- It is about cruelty in the animal world.
- It is about the way the strong pick on the defenceless.
- It shows that even in death the cormorant retains its dignity.
- It is about human beings as much as birds.

Coursework

4 Most people would agree that the story is very bleak. Write a 'happy' version of the last three or four paragraphs. Then write a paragraph explaining what effect this radical change has to the story. Does it lose its power?

The Dress

1 Stop reading at the end of the first paragraph. What do you think is going on? Who is the main character? Who is chasing him? Why is he on the run?

2 Once you have read the whole story, look again at the same questions. Can you answer all of them? In particular, try to work out what the relationship is between the 'madman' and the woman.

3 To clarify the story, hot-seat the man and the young woman. Ask the 'madman' about 'the place he had left', what he was escaping from, his journey, and the woman he is coming to. Ask her about her family, the dress she has made, her feelings when the man arrives at her house.

4 Why do you think the story is called *The Dress*? What is so important about the dress? Look at the different references to it throughout the story.

5 Dylan Thomas's style is a mixture of story-telling and poetry. Look at some of the lively images he uses, and discuss what picture they create in your mind:

IMAGE	PICTURE IN YOUR MIND
the mist was a mother to him	
The world was a ball under his feet	
once he was through the fence, the hosts of the garden came rushing to meet him	
Like a man of blood he came out of the enemy's darkness on to the steps.	

Coursework

6 Look again at the ending of the story. Do you think the man has safely escaped his pursuers, or will he inevitably be caught? Write the next stage in the story, trying to echo the way Dylan Thomas uses language.

The Half-Brothers

1 Reread the early part of the story and imagine what William Preston's proposal to Helen might have been like. What might have been said? How did they both behave? Role-play or write about this moment, showing how stilted and formal it must have been.

2 As you read the story, in what ways did it feel 'old'? Look for some examples of sentences or words which give a hint about the age of the story.

3 Gregory seems badly treated in this story, and we see little from his point of view. What does he think of his treatment by his stepfather and half-brother? Is he proud, bitter, angry? Write as if you were Gregory about your treatment at home and school.

Coursework

4 Mr Preston obviously dies full of regrets for the way he has behaved. Imagine a note or diary account he leaves behind him, discussing what his feelings for his family used to be and what his feelings are now.

5 Which parts of the story do you like and dislike? If you were Elizabeth Gaskell's editor, and she had just sent you this story, what comments and advice would you give? Write a letter to her suggesting alterations in the story-line, characterisation and style of the tale.

Social and historical contexts

- What clues are there in the stories by Liam O'Flaherty, Dylan Thomas and Elizabeth Gaskell about when they were written and what society was like then? Look at references to people and places, technology, clothes, behaviour, expectations and conventions. Look at the language used in each story – does any of it feel rooted in a specific period? Make discussion notes on the way the stories compare and contrast in this way, and on similarities and differences with our own time.

Comparisons

- What similarities and differences can you find in the way the three stories show relationships?
- Which story contains:
  the most cruelty?
  the most disturbing story-line?
  the liveliest style?
  the strongest message?
- Which story do you like best and why?

Bang, Bang – Who's Dead?

1 What impressions do you gain of Fran as you read the story? How does she develop as a character?

2 How would Fran's mother describe her daughter? Interview her.

3 Look again at the matter-of-fact opening to this story. It presents the idea of a ghost in a house as if it were an everyday event. At which point in the story does tension begin to develop? Try to identify an exact starting-point.

Coursework

4 How could Jane Gardam have increased the 'creepiness' of the story? Choose one moment and write it in a way which emphasises the ghost story genre more: pay close attention to description of people and places. Then write a reflective paragraph describing how you worked, what changes you have made and comparing your version with the original.

5 What do you think happens next? Continue the story, using the last extracts of dialogue as your starting-point.

The Signalman

1 Look back at the beginning of the story. At what point does it begin to feel like a ghost story? What are the first hints?

2 'There was something in the man that daunted me.' Write a description of the signalman – his looks, his behaviour, and the strange atmosphere which surrounds him.

3 This is how one reader responded to the story: 'It's a really entertaining ghost story, full of atmosphere and tension. But Dickens completely ruins the effect in his final paragraph. It would be a better story if the last paragraph were left off.' Discuss this in a group. How far do you agree? Is there anything you particularly admire or dislike in the story?

Coursework

4 Imagine how the narrator might be haunted by these events. Could he have done anything to change what happened? Write a diary entry in which he reflects on the strange events on the line and how he might have behaved differently.

5 Is the 'horror' effect of the story made stronger or weaker by the old-fashioned language? How would the tale work in modern English for a modern audience? Choose a moment from the story – perhaps the opening – and rewrite it in a modern style. See what the effect is.

Social and historical contexts

• What clues are there in the stories by Jane Gardam and Charles Dickens about when they were written and what society was like then? Look at references to people and places, technology, clothes, behaviour, expectations and conventions. Look at the language used in each story – does any of it feel rooted in a specific period? Make discussion notes on the way the stories compare and contrast in this way, and on similarities and differences with our own time.

Comparisons

- How do the two main characters in the stories by Gardam and Dickens – Fran and the observer – differ? In what ways are they similar? Make a two-column list to compare them.
- What similarities and differences do you notice in the way the writers create a strong sense of atmosphere?
- Which story do you prefer and why?

The authors

Charles Dickens (1812–70). Dickens's father was imprisoned in a debtors' jail and, aged 12, Dickens worked in a blacking warehouse. Memories of his poverty-stricken childhood run through much of his work. He began his writing career as a parliamentary reporter, writing *Sketches by 'Boz'* and developing his skill for quick characterisation. His first novel, *Pickwick Papers*, was published in twenty monthly instalments and achieved huge popularity. Dickens became a celebrity, each new book eagerly awaited in Britain and (later) in America. He also wrote Christmas specials and short stories for magazines, of which the ghost story *The Signalman* is the most famous.

Jane Gardam (1928–) grew up in Coatham, North Yorkshire, where her father was housemaster at a boy's school for forty-two years. After graduating with a degree in English from Bedford College, London, she became a journalist. Married in 1954 she became a housewife and mother and began to write. Her first collection of short stories, *A Few Fair Days*, was published in 1971. She has written for children and adults, and her novel, *The Queen of the Tambourine*, won the Whitbread Award for novels in 1991. She has also won a variety of awards for her short stories.

Elizabeth Gaskell (1810–65). Elizabeth Cleghorn was brought up by an aunt in Knutsford, Cheshire. In 1832 she married church minister William Gaskell and had four daughters, and a son who died as a child. She began writing in response to her grief at his death, and in 1848 published *Mary Barton*. It caught the attention of Dickens who invited her to write for his magazines. Gaskell was a keen observer of human behaviour, with a sharp ear for the speech patterns of the industrial workers of Manchester and the farming communities of Cheshire.

Graham Greene (1904–91) was born in Hertfordshire and educated at the school where his father was headmaster. He had a deeply disturbed adolescence and 'when boredom reached an intolerable depth' played Russian roulette with his brother's revolver. He went on to read History at Oxford and then worked briefly as a newspaper sub-editor and, later, a film critic. His novels frequently explore questions of divided loyalty and unease about faith. He is also well known for several books of autobiography and travel writing.

Susan Hill (1942–) was born in Scarborough, Yorkshire, after which she was educated at various grammar schools and King's College, London. She published her first novel, *The Enclosure*, at the age of 19 and has earned her living as a novelist ever since. Her works usually have an English setting but are never cosy. Hill often painfully explores the tension and cruelties in human relationships. She is well known for her novels – such as *I'm the King of the Castle* and *Strange Meeting* – and has also won awards for her short stories.

D. H. Lawrence (1885–1930) was born in the mining village of Eastwood, Nottinghamshire, and he lived through a childhood of poverty and friction between his parents. He began his working life as a clerk in a surgical appliance factory; then studied at University College, Nottingham, after which he became a teacher. His frustration with teaching is reflected in the story included in this book, and in 1911 he decided to earn his living as a full-time writer. His novels were popular and often notorious for their depiction of sexual relationships. Ill health plagued him and he travelled extensively abroad in search of warmer weather. He eventually died, aged just 44, in the hills above Nice in France.

Doris Lessing (1919–). Born in Persia (now Iran), Lessing's family moved to Zimbabwe when she was a child. Here she spent her 'hellishly lonely' childhood. She was educated in Britain and describes herself as a 'drop-out, long before the term had been invented'. She became interested in writing at about 14 and has written volumes of autobiography, novels, science fiction and short stories. Her short novel, *The Fifth Child*, is a dark, disturbing tale of a child possessed by evil.

Penelope Lively (1933–). The daughter of a bank manager, Penelope Lively was born in Cairo, where she lived until the age of 12. At this point she was sent to boarding school in Britain; then on to Oxford; then settling near the city to become a full-time writer. She began as a children's novelist – see, for example, *The Ghost of Thomas Kempe* – but has since concentrated upon writing adult fiction. Her novel *Moon Tiger* won the Booker Prize in 1987.

Katherine Mansfield (1888–1923). Born in Wellington, Mansfield frequently used the backdrop of rural New Zealand in her short stories. She came to England in 1903 as a music student and then scraped a living as a writer. Her stories were important in moving the form away from well-made tales to more impressionistic writing – that is, conveying atmosphere and feelings rather than emphasising plot. Her health suffered from around 1914 and, like D. H. Lawrence (whom she was friends with for a time), she travelled to improve her health. She died aged just 34.

V. S. Naipaul (1932–). Born in Trinidad, Vidiadhar Naipaul won one of four 'island scholarships' to Oxford in 1950. On completing his degree he remained in Britain, taking up the career of freelance writer. He has been a broadcaster and reviewer for the BBC. His early novels were chiefly comedies about life in Trinidad, but his more recent works – such as *A Bend in the River* – have vividly shown the bleak conditions for many in the developing world.

Liam O'Flaherty (1896–1984) grew up in extreme poverty in the Aran Islands, near Galway, Ireland. His father was a farmer and fisherman. Wounded in France during World War I, he took on a series of menial jobs in London, sailed to the USA in 1918, and lived as a beachcomber. He returned to Ireland and then London in 1922 where he concentrated on writing. He wrote novels, non-fiction and a play, but he is best known as a writer of short stories.

Edgar Allan Poe (1809–49) was born in Boston, USA and was orphaned at an early age. At six he was brought to England, where he was educated, before returning to the United States where he enlisted in the army. He wrote poems and stories from an early age, and is most famous for his Gothic tales – stories containing our worst nightmares: burial alive, torture and murder. His influence on the horror-fiction genre has been enormous.

Dylan Thomas (1914–53) grew up in Swansea in South Wales where his father was senior English master at the grammar school. On leaving school in 1931 he became a reporter on the South Wales *Evening Post*, before moving to London where his first book of verse, *18 Poems*, made an immediate impact. He became infamous for his reckless life style while in London – heavy drinking and womanising. During the war he became a freelance radio broadcaster and wrote many radio plays – most famously, *Under Milk Wood*. During a lecture tour of the USA, he collapsed of alcoholic poisoning and died shortly afterwards.

Further reading

Charles Dickens, *Selected Shorter Fiction* (Penguin, 1976)
Dickens's short fiction has a very different feel from his novels, not just because it's briefer, but there's also a sense of a major artist writing to entertain a loyal readership – many of his stories were written especially for his magazine readers at Christmas. Several have a supernatural theme.

Jane Gardam, *Showing the Flag* (Abacus, 1990)
Gardam is known for her children's and adult novels. She is also a terrific short-story writer, often dealing with childhood views of the adult world.

Elizabeth Gaskell, *North and South* (1855)
Gaskell wrote short stories for magazine publication but is best remembered for her novels of working life, such as this one.

Graham Greene, *Collected Short Stories* (Penguin, 1981)
Greene was a prolific author of novels and short stories. Many of them deal with similar themes – guilt, cruelty, despair. That may sound like a catalogue of bleak reading matter, yet his work is frequently funny too.

Susan Hill, *The Elephant Man and Other Stories* (Penguin, 1974)
Hill is well known for her short stories – the above collection is well worth reading – and you may enjoy her novels, such as *Strange Meeting*, about a friendship in World War I, and *I'm the King of the Castle*, a lesson in cruelty, and her choice of *Ghost Stories*. All three are in Longman Imprint Books.

D. H. Lawrence, *The Mortal Coil and Other Stories* (Penguin, 1971)
Sixteen short stories written when Lawrence was in his twenties. Several deal with his frustration as a schoolteacher.

Doris Lessing, *To Room Nineteen* (Flamingo, 1994) and *Collected African Stories* I and II (Paladin, 1992)
Doris Lessing's writing is distinguished by a wonderful clear style. These collections show some of her best short-story writing. You might also enjoy her horror story, *The Fifth Child* (Longman Literature).

Penelope Lively, *Pack of Cards and Other Stories* (Penguin, 1987)
A comprehensive selection of stories from one of our leading novelists.

Katherine Mansfield, *Collected Stories* (Penguin, 1981)
This comprehensive collection shows the talent of Katherine Mansfield to evoke the atmosphere of people and places.

V. S. Naipaul, *A Flag on the Island* (Penguin, 1969)
A lively collection of tales set in the West Indies and London.

Liam O'Flaherty, *The Short Stories of Liam O'Flaherty* (New English Library, 1961)
O'Flaherty's stories are frequently very short, but they brilliantly capture precise moments in their subjects' lives. This is an excellent introduction to his work.

Edgar Allan Poe, *Selected Writings* (Penguin, 1967)
Poe is best remembered for his horror stories, and this collection contains all the most famous examples.

Dylan Thomas, *Adventures in the Skin Trade* (Dent, 1955)
Thomas·is famed for his poetry and lively drama. His short
stories – like *The Dress* – show his power of story-telling and
creating memorable atmosphere.

Further reading projects

1 Choose a short story you particularly like and rewrite it
through the eyes of a different character. Imagine, for
example, *Through the Tunnel* told from the viewpoint of
Jerry's mother.

2 Based on your own wider reading, put together your own
anthology of four or five favourite stories. Then write an
introduction for a new reader, saying why you chose them,
what you like about them and some comments about the
authors' styles.